KILLING IMAGINARY FRIENDS

ARDELLE HOLDEN

Holden

Book One

ISBN

978-1-990523-05-2 Audiobook

978-1-990523-04-5 Hardcover Book

978-1-990523-03-8 Paperback Book

978-1-990523-02-1 Electronic Book

Dedicated to Patrick
the love of my life

ONE

WHAT A CRAPPY BIRTHDAY. Olly's eyes burned with tears. He stumbled up the stairs, back to bed, his pajama sleeve wet and cold against his nose. Even with the storm outside and his door closed, their angry voices pierced his ears. His Iron Man pillow wrapped tight around his ears wasn't much help either, but it smothered his sobs. Deep under the covers, he hunched his shoulders as high and hard as they would go. His breath struggled past the lump in his throat.

A door slammed. *Mom's really mad at him now.*

He had woken Olly out of a sound sleep with his bellowing. "Olly. Hey. Olly. Wake up. Come on down and blow out your candles again." Groggy, Olly had rubbed his eyes and shuffled downstairs, the floor cold on his bare feet. He pretended not to notice the beer on his dad's breath when he hugged him, but he couldn't help pulling away. The stubby candles looked stupid in the lopsided, leftover cake. When Olly blew, a little spit came out. Even though his mom shook her head and mouthed, *It's okay*, his cheeks felt hot. His dad hadn't even noticed, but then, he never noticed even when Olly did things right.

"Sorry I'm late, Olly. Eight years old, eh? Wow, you're getting to be a big boy." He slapped Olly's shoulder awkwardly and flopped onto the sofa. "What'd you get for your birthday?"

Olly looked at his mother. She had said the Lego was from her *and* him. She mouthed, *I'm sorry.* But it didn't matter. His dad didn't even say good night when she sent him back to bed.

He squeezed the pillow tighter around his ears. *It's okay, Mom, just stop fighting.* But she couldn't hear his thoughts. The sound of his own breathing muffled their voices a little.

"How could you do this to Olly? You knew it was his birthday. This is the last straw, Curtis."

"For chrissake, Lauren. It's Friday night. We just went for a few drinks after work, and I lost track of time."

"Couldn't you have made an exception tonight? And who is *we?*"

His father's boozy voice thundered through the pillow. "Just someone from work. Get a grip, Lauren. He'll get over it."

"But why tonight of all nights? And since when does happy hour last four hours? If I didn't know better, I'd think it was a woman."

Dead silence. Olly uncovered his head, sat up, and leaned toward the door. His father mumbled something.

"I knew it. How long has this been going on? Don't tell me: since June, when you went to Vancouver—alone. Right?"

More mumbling. Olly could tell his mother was crying. He didn't want to hear more, but when her voice grew quiet, he crept out of bed and listened at the crack in the door.

"You can't hurt me any more than you already have, Curtis, but this is the last time you'll disappoint Olly. We're out of here."

What? Olly jumped back into bed and pulled the covers over his head. The sound of stomping on the stairs competed with his halting breath, his heartbeat, and the rain against the window. It was hard not to snuffle. He peeked out and saw his mother's thin frame silhouetted in the doorway. "Mom?"

"Yes, Olly. Get dressed." Her voice was strained. In the dim light, she placed his brand-new box of Lego at the bottom of his backpack and opened his dresser drawer. "We'll just take a few clothes."

He stared at her, hardly blinking as he pulled his pajama top over his head. He fumbled with the zipper on his jeans.

Branches scratched against the window like angry fingernails. He dashed to smack the light switch on. The room flooded with light, but his heart still raced. Even squinting against the harsh light, he could see his mother had been crying.

His eyes darted between his mother's stoic expression and the battered window. "The storm is really bad, Mom. Where are we going?"

"We're going to visit Aunt Lila." She rammed pajamas, some T-shirts, jeans, and underwear into his backpack. His eyes grew wide at the sight of her neat folding undone so carelessly. She helped him wrestle his backpack over his jacket without a word and led him down the hall to their bedroom. When she pulled her suitcase off the top shelf of the closet, she swung it onto her bed with the fury of a hammer thrower. Olly backed away. She was really, really mad this time. Without a word, he watched her ram a jumble of clothes into the suitcase: skinny jeans and T-shirts, mostly, and some underwear. A breeze blew back his hair when she swept past him into her bathroom. Bottles and jars clanked into her purse from the counter. When she held up a new toothbrush for him, she forced a smile—he could tell. "Turn around, and I'll tuck it in your backpack."

With her collar pulled over her long black curls, she cinched her coat belt around her tiny waist and frowned at her runners. "Ready, dear? Let's brave the storm." As if on cue, thunder rolled. Olly followed her suitcase as it bumped down the stairs. His mom didn't even spare a sideways glance at his dad, passed out on the sofa, but Olly couldn't help it. His dad's dark hair was all messed up, his tie undone, his shirt untucked. "Sorry, Dad." But there was no reply— just a snort from his open mouth.

* * *

THE RAIN HIT Olly's face like a blasting cold shower. He dashed to the car and jumped into the back seat. Shivering, with his fists jammed into his jacket pockets, he bit his bottom lip and stared into the rearview mirror. The street lights lit up his mother's face as they passed. Wet hair hung across her cheek, but it didn't hide her tears. When they came to Goldstream Park, she leaned into the wheel— her eyes riveted on the darkness ahead. The windshield wipers slapped against the pounding rain and squeaked like a trapped animal. How could she see? They drove in silence up, up to the summit. The trees on the mountainside swayed; their branches flapped at him with the fury of massive eagle wings. He peered through the swirling rain into the darkness on the other side of the highway, where the ocean waited for drunk drivers... and people who drove in storms when they should have stayed home. A cold worm of sweat trickled down his neck. He could only whisper. "How much farther to Auntie Lila's?"

"Not long now. We're almost over the Malahat, but... Oh, god." The car slowed.

Olly craned his neck to see ahead. Flashing lights lit up the rain-streaked windows and stabbed the blackness of the night. "What is it, Mom? Why are we stopping?"

"It's an accident. Keep your head down, dear."

But he couldn't help it. He wiped his breath off the window and pressed his nose against the cold glass. His head jerked back when the wind threw a bucket of rain at his face. He swallowed hard. His heart pounded in his ears. Flashes of color streaked across the wet road—red, blue, red, blue.

Then, against the cruiser lights, a yellow raincoat directed them, its flashlight casting brilliant arcs in the sky. They crept past a crumpled car lying upside down on the shoulder. Shattered glass, strewn everywhere, glared red and blue.

Olly couldn't blink, and he didn't dare breathe or he would fog up the window again. A little boy... in his pj's... lying on the road... with a teddy bear. The rain beating on his face didn't even make him blink. Their car crept on. *Wait! No!* Olly spread his hands on the window, almost pushing his forehead through the glass, but the little boy's eyes disappeared under a ghostly white sheet behind other yellow raincoats. Olly slumped forward in his seat as the tightness in his chest crept up his neck. He closed his eyes and pressed his fists against his ears. *Could be me.* The little boy, his eyes, his teddy bear, his cold and wet body: Olly could see it all, as if it were burned with a laser inside his eyelids. His mom drove slowly away, deserting the boy. Olly twisted in his seat to look out the back window, but the flashing lights chased them away. Nothing he could do. He fought the tears that had so many excuses to spill tonight.

"Oliver, get your face away from that window."

"I'm not looking anymore."

He pulled his head inside his steamy jacket. It was just a little lie. She was sad enough. He squeezed his eyes shut again, but, in his mind, the little boy was still staring. *If only I could be his friend—help him somehow. Poor little kid—all alone out there. I'll bet he's dead.*

A small voice whispered, *Prob'ly. I still have my teddy. He's all wet and yucky, just like me, but I can be your friend too.*

Olly's head popped out of his cozy jacket shell, and his gaze froze on the little boy sitting beside him. The little guy shrugged and hugged his soggy teddy bear. Olly blinked, and blinked again. "How... how did you get here?" As soon as the words were out, he slapped his hand over his mouth. His eyes darted to the rearview mirror. Panic squeezed his throat.

But his mom just leaned over the wheel and peered into the darkness beyond the headlights. "What did you say, Olly?"

"Nothing. Just wondering who that was in that accident." Again, the little boy just shrugged. That was no help.

"Did you see someone back there?"

Olly's heart almost jumped out of his chest when his mother looked at him in the mirror, but she didn't see the little kid sitting right beside him. "No one, just... uh, a teddy bear on the road." He cringed. *I shouldn't have said that.* He opened one eye to check the boy. Still there.

"Oh, Olly. You weren't supposed to look. It might give you nightmares."

"No duh." Olly yanked his eyes away from the kid when his mom glanced at him again.

Like a thug in a back alley, Olly whispered out of the side of his mouth, his eyes darting from the mirror to the kid. "Are you okay?"

The boy looked down at his pj's. *I guess so.* His voice seemed loud in Olly's head, but his mom didn't seem to hear it.

Again, Olly checked the mirror. *Nope. She can't see him, and she can't hear him—maybe.*

Olly zipped up his mouth with his fingers, and the boy did the same.

* * *

WHEN HIS MOM pulled into Aunt Lila's driveway, Olly rolled his eyes and exhaled until he figured he was empty. His aunt stood in the doorway, black against the light, hugging herself.

His mother dropped her head against the wheel when she turned off the engine. Olly flinched and grabbed her shoulder. "Are you all right, Mom?"

"Yes, dear. I'm just tired and glad we made it safely."

Olly's stomach did a little flip. Arriving safely was not his biggest problem. The kid still sat beside him and still stared at him. Maybe he would stay in the car. Or disappear.

Olly closed his eyes and wished him away. He opened them, and —poof—the kid was gone. But Olly's sigh of relief choked off. There was the kid, sneaking around Aunt Lila's legs into the house. Olly blinked the rain from his eyes as they darted from his mom to Aunt Lila. For a second, he held his breath. Couldn't they see him? They just kept talking about the rain. Olly buzzed his lips as he exhaled. *Guess not.* He rolled his eyes, grabbed his backpack, and jumped out into the rain.

His mom slammed the door behind him and guided him up the darkened walk. The water pouring off the roof would have drowned out her voice if she hadn't yelled close to his ear. "Let's get you out of the rain."

Inside the familiar foyer, Olly stomped on the mat while his aunt peeled off his steamy jacket. The smell of his warm sweat wafted up between them. He wrinkled his nose and checked her face. But she was cool—never even mentioned it. She shook the wet off his coat and hung it on a hook behind the door.

"What a night to have to drive the Malahat. I figured you'd be late. You must be tired."

Olly shivered. "You should have seen the big accident on the road. There was a car upside down, and I saw a… a teddy bear on the road." The boy sat at the bottom of the staircase, hugging his soggy bear and nodding.

Aunt Lila gasped, and his mother shook her head. "I'll tell you about it later. Right now, I just need to bring in my bag." She dropped her purse, pulled her hood up and around her chin, and ducked back out into the rain.

His aunt's expression turned from shock to a smile as she gave his hand a warm squeeze. "Come on. I've got your room all fixed up for you. I'll bring you some hot chocolate." A quick glance at Aunt Lila told him she didn't see the boy sitting right there in front of her.

They squeezed side by side on the stairs. Olly carried his backpack in front of him, because his mom was right: her "big" sister was definitely "big-boned."

Olly almost said, "Get out of the way," but the little boy was already dragging his teddy bear up the last few steps. Disaster averted.

* * *

AUNT LILA USHERED Olly into the spare bedroom he and his mom used to share when they visited before Uncle Arthur died. His dad never stayed overnight. Now Brad's old *Star Wars* curtains hung on the window, his old toys sat on the shelves, and a scruffy-looking bear, much like the boy's, leaned against the pillow. An uneasy feeling crept over him. *Brad. Such a big shot, just because he's eighteen.*

When a door down the hall opened, Olly jumped, but Brad just rubbed his eyes and shuffled to the bathroom without a glance into the room. *Good.* The less Brad noticed him, the better. Olly wasn't going to mention, ever, that Brad still had all this kid stuff.

"Well, here we are. This will be your room. I've brought down some of Brad's things from when he was your age. You can replace them with yours when they come."

Olly swallowed the dread that clogged his throat. "I don't think we'll be staying that long, Aunt Lila. I've just got my overnight stuff in my backpack."

Aunt Lila raised her eyebrows and flicked her raven curls over her shoulder just as his mom entered the room. "Lauren. He doesn't know?"

His mom shook her head and waved Aunt Lila off.

"What don't I know, Mom?" Her last words to his dad echoed in his brain. *We're out of here.*

She shook her head and pushed the wet hair off his forehead. "It's late, dear. Get into your pajamas, brush your teeth, and dry your hair. I'll look in before I go to bed." She hugged him. "Leave your wet things in the bathroom." She kissed his cheek and followed her sister out the door.

"Wait, Mom." Olly rushed to her and wrapped his arms around her waist. "Where are you going to sleep?" Her heart beat softly in his ear.

She stroked his wet hair. "I'm going to sleep in Aunt Lila's room. Will you be okay in here alone?"

"I guess." But it wasn't okay. She hugged him and stroked his back the way she always did when Dad broke a promise. He tried to smile—for her.

The boy dodged around them into the room, startling Olly.

His mom lifted his face up by the chin. "You shivered. You'd better get out of those wet clothes."

"I'll be okay, Mom. Good night." He broke away from her and

plunked his backpack on the bed. The door closed with a quiet click, leaving him alone… except for… He glanced at the kid.

Olly's chest felt tight. He slumped down on the bed next to his backpack. He tried to ignore this grungy little guy leaning on the bed with his chin in his hands and staring at him with puppy dog eyes.

Olly yawned and dumped out his backpack. The Lego box was now on top of the heap. "Do you want to play with my new Legos?" Olly emptied the box on the carpet. The boy smiled from ear to ear and plopped down beside them. Soon he was fishing around in the pile for the little people. Olly smiled; those were his favorite pieces too.

"What's your name, anyway?"

The boy shrugged. *I dunno. Who are you?*

"Oliver, but you can call me Olly." He perched on the end of the bed, watching. Just in case anyone was listening in the hall, he thought, *I think I'll call you PJ. Would you like that?* The boy didn't seem to hear him. "I said, I think I'll call you PJ. Would you like that?"

The boy smiled up at him and nodded. He held up a whole little Lego person for Olly's approval. *This looks like my mommy. Is she still in the car with Daddy?*

Olly looked away; he figured PJ would ask something like this, and he didn't know what to say. "Maybe. I don't know, PJ." Olly handed the Lego lady back to PJ. "Hey. Do you know how old you are?"

PJ held up three and then four fingers. *Three or four? I dunno.*

"Boy, you sure don't know much."

PJ went back to playing. He seemed to have lost interest in finding his mom and dad. He popped another head on a body without looking up. Relieved, Olly rolled his eyes. "Whatever." He'd better look out for PJ—keep the kid from getting scared. *His mom and dad aren't just mad for a few days. They're probably dead.*

Olly scooped his clothes off the bed and, except for his pajamas, dumped them in an empty drawer. He yawned. *Must be after midnight.* For the third time that night, he was going to bed. Now it wasn't even his own bed. Even worse, it looked like Brad's.

As he undressed, he glanced at PJ playing quietly with the Lego. He headed for the bathroom.

He scowled at himself in the mirror. It seemed like days, not hours, since he'd said goodbye to his friends after the party. He stifled the panicky voice in his head that wondered when he would see them again. But now he had a new friend, even if he was only imaginary. Olly fought back tears as he struggled to get the new toothbrush out of the package. Even the toothpaste wouldn't cooperate. He squeezed out way too much and groaned when it fell off into the sink. He growled, trying to brush his teeth with his face all puckered up. *What else can go wrong today?*

At the thought of PJ, he appeared, sitting on the edge of the tub.

Whoa! Olly almost choked.

PJ just stared.

"You still can't hear me unless I talk out loud?" Olly sputtered through the toothpaste, rinsed, and spat. "Don't sneak up on me like that." PJ looked up at him like a little brother would. If he were PJ's big brother, he would never be mean like Brad, but he had to be firm. "And don't use my toothbrush." That was only fair.

PJ nodded and hugged his bear. *That's okay. I prob'ly already brushed 'cause I'm in my jammies.*

"Yeah, I guess so." Olly cocked his head to one side with his hands on his hips. "In my head, you talk like my friend Jeff's little brother. I guess that's okay since I don't know what you really talk like. I wonder what Jeff would think if he knew about you."

Olly shut off the light and headed back to his bedroom. "Come on."

PJ trundled behind him as if he were on a leash, and struggled to climb onto the bed.

"You can't sleep under the covers. You're all wet and dirty. Better get off." PJ scampered to the floor. Olly ran his hand over Brad's *Star Wars* blanket, but it wasn't wet, or dirty, or even wrinkled. He shrugged. "Well, I guess it's okay. It doesn't rub off." He turned back the covers and PJ climbed in, warming Olly with a big-brother kind of feeling.

Jarring him back into reality, his mother rapped on the door and came in. "Who are you talking to, Olly?"

Olly grabbed Brad's old bear and jammed it under the covers beside PJ. "Uh, just this old bear. He's probably been in a box for years." He rolled his eyes under his eyelids. *Quick thinking, genius.*

She sat beside him and tucked him in. "You are such a considerate boy, Olly. Everybody needs a friend like you." She bent over and kissed him on the forehead. "Good night, dear."

"Good night, Mom." But before she closed the door, he had to ask. "Why does Auntie Lila think I'm bringing all my stuff up here?"

She sighed and placed her praying hands against her lips. "We're going to be staying here for a while. It's very late, Olly, so you get some sleep, and we'll talk about it in the morning. Okay? I love you." She eased the door closed behind her.

Olly yawned and snuggled down beside his new imaginary friend. "Mom doesn't seem so upset now. What do you think?"

PJ shrugged. *Maybe this isn't so bad.*

"Exactly what I was thinking. I wonder how long 'a while' is."

TWO

OLLY'S EYES fluttered open to a room that wasn't his. He hadn't dreamed that part. But was PJ real? He turned his head, and there he was—hugging that bedraggled teddy bear, and he still looked wet. Olly frowned and shook his head. He squeezed his eyes shut and snapped them open again. "Why are you still here?" Frustration clouded his voice.

I dunno. Are mommy and daddy still in the car?

"I don't really know who was in the car with you. I'm just guessing."

Like the night before, he could hear PJ's voice in his head— or was he just imagining it? But it didn't matter. It was just cool to have a friend, even an imaginary one.

Olly yawned and pulled the covers over his head. "Let me explain something. Yesterday, I was eight, and my dad forgot, so Mom got really upset and we left in that storm last night. I guess that's not as bad as your accident, but still… it was a crappy day and even crappier night. I'm still tired." Olly threw back the covers and jumped out of bed. He pulled his pajama top over his head, just about ripping his ears off.

"Ow."

He stared at the Lego scattered on the floor, just the way they'd come out of the box. "I guess you didn't really play with these last night." He kicked a block across the room. "I know the Legos were just from Mom. Dad didn't even know what I got."

His mother's voice drifted up from downstairs. "Olly, come and have your breakfast."

He pulled on his jeans and talked through his T-shirt like a headless boy. "Mom and Dad had a really big fight last night, so she's really sad. And I wasn't supposed to look out and see the accident last night." His head popped through the neck hole. He liked doing that. "I'm the only one who can see you, so I can't tell her about you. She'd freak out. You'd better stay up here. Okay? And be quiet."

PJ nodded.

Olly was going to have to look out for PJ—the kid didn't even know his own name.

* * *

AT THE BOTTOM of the stairs, Brad sneered and swung his backpack over his shoulder, bumping Olly in the head. "Watch where you're going, squirt." He swaggered toward the door, turning his lanky body to glance back and scoff. His black stringy hair hung over one eye.

Squirt wasn't what Brad called him when there were no adults around. Olly rubbed his head. *That was on purpose.*

Aunt Lila clicked her tongue from the kitchen. "Be nice, Brad. You're going into your senior year. Don't you think it's time you grew up?" But the door slammed on her words. She cleared away his bowl, making it clatter in the sink. "Sorry about that, Olly."

Olly stepped off the bottom step toe first, as if he were checking to see how cold the water was. It was cold today. He exhaled and dragged his feet into the kitchen.

Aunt Lila couldn't keep Brad from picking on him. Brad was mad at the whole world, Olly included. He'd better steer clear… but for how long?

Aunt Lila threw her tea towel over her shoulder and shrugged in Olly's direction. *Poor Auntie. Brad's such a jerk.*

His mother's black satin hair shone in the morning sun streaming through the bay window behind her. She didn't look as sad this morning. That was good.

She patted the chair beside her. "Come and sit by me, Olly. We need to talk."

He cringed a little inside. Maybe he didn't want to hear this. He stirred in the cinnamon his mother always sprinkled on top of his cereal, and dawdled as long as he could, swinging his legs in time with the clock. *A clock that ticks—that's funny.*

His mom's voice interrupted the clock. "You like visiting your Aunt Lila, don't you, Olly?"

"Sure. It's okay." He squished a raisin to the bottom of his bowl. *That's Brad.*

"Well, dear… we're going to be staying here for a lot longer this time."

A lot longer? Olly could almost feel Brad giving him a wedgie. He made a fist around his spoon. "Is it because Dad forgot my birthday and blew his beer breath all over my cake? 'Cause I don't care about that."

"No. I guess you'd call that the straw that broke the camel's back."

Olly stuffed his mouth with cereal and chewed till it was mush. When he snickered, it almost came out of his nose. "You always say that, Mom. Don't you mean 'the icing on the cake' this time?" He paused. "You know. My birthday cake?" He waited, squeezing a sassy question mark between his eyebrows. Even Aunt Lila, who was leaning against the kitchen sink, stood with her mouth hanging open. But then his mom threw back her head and laughed so hard she cried. Lila gave Olly a wink and joined in with gut-splitting howls. Olly exhaled and rolled his eyes.

The laughter turned to sighs. "Oh, Olly. I needed that." His mom stroked his arm, and he listened to a lot of uncomfortable dead air before she spoke again. "The thing is… your dad and I have been unhappy together for some time now, so we've decided to live apart." She rubbed Olly's shoulder while he ate. "It doesn't mean we both don't love you."

Olly looked up into the same sad eyes he saw every time his dad did something stupid. His joke had worn off already. "So Dad knows about this living apart thing? He'll be all alone? When will I see him?" It was getting harder and harder to hold back the tears.

"Your dad will be fine, Olly. And you'll visit him whenever you want, so he won't be lonely." She wrapped her arms around him and kissed the top of his head. "Are you going to be all right?"

"Sure, Mom." He took another huge mouthful of cereal, so he didn't have to talk—or lie—anymore.

His mother pushed the hair out of his eyes and smiled. "I'm so sorry, dear. I've been wrestling with this decision for a long time."

Olly's head spun. "You knew we were coming to Aunt Lila's before?"

"Yes, dear. But I wanted all of us to be together one last time on your birthday. I'm sorry we left the way we did. I had hoped we would drive up this weekend. It's important that you get settled in before school starts."

Oliver's stomach flipped. "School—here? In Nanaimo?"

THREE

BRAD HADN'T GIVEN OLLY MORE than a grunt in passing since they'd moved in two weeks earlier, but that was okay with Olly. *The jerk is even mean to his own mom.* As if it were her fault they had to stay here.

It was the first day of school, and Aunt Lila stood in the doorway, her fists jammed into her hips. "Brad, this is Olly's first day in a new school. The least you can do is bike with him. You're going that way anyway."

Olly stiffened in horror. *No, no, no, no.* Brad would pick on him more than anyone else.

"I don't want him tagging along with me." Brad glared at him. "You can't even keep up."

"It's okay, Aunt Lila. I know how to get to the school on my own. I've biked past there lots of times. Pleeeeze?"

Aunt Lila scowled at Brad. "Well, if you think you can get there on your own, Olly, I'll let you go, but you be back here within fifteen minutes of that bell this afternoon, or I'll have to answer to your mother."

Brad brushed past Olly, whispering "pissant" under his breath.

His back tire spit grit off the driveway in Olly's direction as he sped away.

Olly mounted his bike and waved goodbye to his aunt. He wasn't going to let Brad think he was afraid just because it was a new school. *Why couldn't Mom be late for work, just this once?* His tires went *flubbidy-flub* over the cracks in the sidewalk, just like they had with his friends back home. He huffed and spun his tires, almost losing control but recovering like a pro. Back home, his friend Jeff would have been impressed.

At the entrance to the park, he sighed. "Well, here goes." For the first time, he wouldn't be biking through this park just for fun. Leaves fluttered and curled around him, stirred up by the other kids speeding past. Maybe he'd cut off to the pond and hang out there all day. Nobody would miss him. Then again, if he ditched, he'd prob-ably have to bike to school with Brad *forever*. He pushed himself to bypass the pond. When the school came into view at the edge of the park, he slowed to a stop. Two kids almost plowed into him from behind. "Hey. Don't stop in the middle of the path, moron." Others giggled as they swerved around him. His heart sank. *If only Dad had come home on time for my birthday.*

* * *

OLLY PARKED his bike in the rack alongside the others and trudged up the sidewalk to the door just as the bell rang. The other kids jostled and bumped him as they rushed to their desks. He hung back, watching them bubble over with excitement as they unloaded fresh school supplies into their desks. He wished he could crawl under one of them.

The teacher approached him with a gentle smile. "Hello. You must be Oliver. I'm Mrs. Donnelly. Welcome to grade three. Here's your desk. Everyone, this is Oliver. He's new from Victoria. Please make him welcome." Nobody laughed. *Maybe this won't be so bad.*

The day progressed without incident until Mrs. Donnelly started reading a question in math about a car going one hundred kilometers an hour. How long would it take to get to Victoria? That night in the rain came flooding back, the crash scene vivid in his brain. Suddenly, PJ was sitting in the aisle, staring at him. Olly almost jumped out of his skin.

Wide-eyed, he whisper-screamed and waved at PJ to disappear. "PJ! What are you doing here? You were supposed to stay home!"

Mrs. Donnelly closed her textbook. "What's that, Oliver?"

Olly's cheeks felt beetroot red. "Uh, nothing, Mrs. Donnelly. Sorry."

The kids around him waved their arms and chanted, "Go home, PJ!" But PJ wouldn't leave. Olly tried to shoo him away with hand gestures under his desk, but the kids saw that too. It was hopeless. The whole class was laughing at him. They mimicked his wide-eyed gestures and whispers. Pretending they could see PJ too, they declared whatever it was, it had to be a fairy—a declaration that would stick to Olly like Elmer's glue.

Mercifully, Mrs. Donnelly came to his rescue and made them quiet down, but the cupped whispers and sideways glances could not be stopped. His ears burned.

* * *

WHEN THE FINAL BELL RANG, Olly couldn't get out of that schoolyard fast enough. He was glad it was raining. No one would see his tears. The wind tore through the trees and plastered dead leaves against his face with a slap. He slammed on his brakes, skidding out of control. When he fell, his bike pinned his leg to the ground. He wished it were a sinkhole to the center of the earth.

The high-school kids zipped around him, laughing and berating him for blocking the trail. It got even worse when a girl, a *high-school girl*, stopped and lifted his bike off his leg. Just when he thought his life couldn't get any worse, he saw PJ standing beside her. Olly bit his tongue to keep from yelling at him.

Her long hair fell in his face when she leaned over and yanked him to his feet. "Are you okay?"

Olly's throat closed up on him. He could only nod as he swiped the wet leaves from his pants, her voice chirping happily in his ear.

"That was, like, choreographed. It was so smooth."

Her compliment drowned in his humiliation. If only PJ hadn't shown up in class, he wouldn't be such a laughingstock. "Don't you ever follow me to school again. Do you hear me?"

Confusion clouded the girl's face. "Excuse me. I wasn't following you. Geez. Some thanks I get for helping you."

"I'm sorry. I wasn't talking to you." Olly felt the heat in his cheeks rise.

She looked around at the stream of babbling kids rushing past. Some of them pointed and giggled.

She put her hands on her hips and squinted at them. "Maybe one of those girls has a crush on you?"

"What? No way. It was someone else." He could have cut out his tongue. There seemed to be no end to his mortification.

The girl threw her hands up in fake exaggeration. "If you say so. What's your name?"

"Oliver, but everyone calls me Olly." He couldn't believe this pretty girl was still walking beside him. His palms were making his handlebars slick. "Uh. What's yours?"

"Alexis, but everyone calls me Alex. Where do you live?"

"On Dufferin."

"No way! So do I. We'll probably see each other a lot on this trail."

Olly couldn't even feel the cold rain anymore. The blonde hair plastered against Alex's face made her look like one of those bathing-suit models. And before he knew it, they were in front of Aunt Lila's house.

Brad whipped around them and into their driveway just as they stopped. "What are you doing with this little pissant, Alex? Or was it just an excuse to see me?"

KILLING IMAGINARY FRIENDS

"As if, Brad." Alex rolled her eyes and turned her back to him.

Olly's tongue got lost in his mouth. He couldn't speak.

Alex smiled at him and skipped down the sidewalk. "Maybe I'll follow you to school tomorrow to see who's stalking you."

FOUR

OLLY GAZED out the classroom window at the dreary sky. It was almost Christmas, and he hadn't seen his dad since Thanksgiving—his first escape from Brad.

What a bummer of a holiday that was. All his stuff was gone from his room; it was now his dad's office. Olly had to sleep on a hide-a-lump for guests. *Guests.* He was a guest in his own room. There had been no Thanksgiving decorations or carved pumpkins on the steps outside, and to top it all off, they'd gone out to a restaurant with some lady. They didn't even have crackers with party hats and prizes inside.

Before, when he and his mom lived there, they'd stuffed the biggest turkey in the world. He rubbed his hands together the way he and his mom had rubbed a whole loaf of white bread into small lumps. He could almost smell the stuffing and feel the cranberries in it when he plunged a fistful into the turkey's backside. That was fun. Aunt Lila, Uncle Art, and Brad had always come down for that. Brad wasn't such an asshole then. *Things will never be good again. Dad's gonna sell my home. Maybe it isn't even my home anymore.* But Aunt Lila's wasn't home either. Olly sighed. *Yup. I'm homeless.*

His teacher slammed her textbook on her desk. "Olly, did you hear what I said?"

"Sorry." He could have crawled under his desk when everyone laughed. So much for stuffing a turkey.

"Who will be your guests at the concert next week?"

"Probably the fairies he's always talking to," some girl at the back of the class piped up amidst the laughter.

"Now, class, that's enough. Olly?"

"Uh, I guess my mom and my aunt." He had to repeat it over the taunts. He laid his head on his desk and closed his eyes.

When he opened them, one girl, Sidney, looked his way. She wasn't laughing like the others; she never did. A questioning frown crossed her face when Olly scowled at PJ under her desk.

At recess, he could avoid the other kids if he stood by the office window. No one teased him there. But Sidney was still looking at him. He glared at PJ playing with pebbles at his feet. "Keep quiet."

PJ's words popped into Olly's head. *I didn't say anything.*

Olly tried talking without moving his lips. "She's coming this way. Oh, no. Is she going to talk to me? Why? What will I say?" Olly clapped his hands over his mouth to make himself stop talking.

PJ stared up at him. *Stop asking me stuff if I can't talk.*

Sidney stopped in front of him with her back to the others. "Hi. Those kids are mean. I know who you're talking to."

Olly's heart thumped. "You do?" He glanced around to see if any of the other kids could hear them. That would be a disaster.

"Yeah. I talk to my stepmother like that all the time. I say all the things I wish I could say to her face. My dad won't listen, so that's what I do."

PJ played in the dirt at his feet, thinking nothing. Olly's heart was doing flips. "Is she dead?"

"No. But sometimes I wish she was."

Another survey of the schoolyard and all was clear—no kids within earshot.

Olly uncurled his finger at PJ. "Well, this kid really is dead."

Sid looked at the ground where he had pointed. "Wow. Was he your brother?"

"No, just some little kid that got killed in a car accident. I saw him on the road. And since then, he's been like an imaginary friend."

"That's awful. What does he look like? Is he bloody and everything?"

Olly cringed. That thought hadn't occurred to him. "No. But it was raining really hard, so his pajamas are all muddy and wet, and his teddy bear too. I call him PJ."

Sid nodded, making her tight brown curls bounce. "'Cause he's in his pajamas, right?"

"Yeah. He doesn't know his name. Well, *I* don't know his name."

Sidney's mouth hung open. "Wow."

"Yeah. You can say that again. Does your stepmother say what you're thinking?

"That's the best part. I can make her say whatever I want."

"Cool. I guess that's what I do too. I just can't control when he pops up."

Sid scowled and fist-bumped Olly. "That's a problem, for sure."

The bell rang to go back in. Olly smiled at PJ and whispered, "I have a friend, and she's just like me."

* * *

THAT AFTERNOON, time dragged for Olly. When the final bell rang, kids, books, shoes, and coats flew in every direction. He stood like a sloth on the road until the stampede had passed. Ever since recess, he'd been on cloud nine. The other kids hadn't teased him, and he hadn't thought of PJ once. Sidney sat one row over from him, and made eye contact a couple of times—knowing glances between confidants.

He zipped his coat up to his throat. Despite the cold, he had a warm feeling inside as he waited by his bike. Sid had parked her bike right next to his, and they were the only two still on the rack.

When she sauntered out the door, swinging her pink backpack over her shoulder, he gulped.

"Hi, Sid." His cheeks got warm when she smiled at him. Her brunette hair stuck out willy-nilly from under her pink tasseled toque.

* * *

SID WALKED her bike out the back gate beside him. His head pivoted from her to the corner and back again until she bumped her front wheel into his. "What's up, Olly?"

"Huh? Oh. I want you to meet someone. She should be here any minute."

They didn't have long to wait. Alex rounded the corner from the high school with Georgia, her so-called friend. Olly avoided eye contact with her. He rolled his eyes so that only Sid would see. "Georgia's a phony. She teases me when Alex isn't around."

Sid nodded like any good co-conspirator would.

Georgia looked down her nose at Olly and turned towards Connie's Café with an over-the-shoulder glance at Alex. "Catch you tomorrow."

Alex nodded and sidled up beside Olly. "Who's your friend?"

"Uh, this is Sid. She's in my class."

"Hi, Sid. You aren't one of the bullies, are you?" Alex's eyes twinkled.

"No way. We got stuff in common." Sid's bike wobbled, so she balanced with her toes on the ground.

"Stupendous. Like what?" Alex nodded at some high-school kids jogging past.

"We both talk to the dead, or the ones we wish were dead." Still touching the ground with her toes, Sid waggled her head, making the pink pom-pom on her toque bob.

Olly shook his head at Alex. His eyeballs felt like they were going to pop out of his head. *Oh, no.*

Alex grinned at him. "It's okay, Olly. I do too." She waved her arms in the air and spun around to smile at the joggers. "We're all freaks." They half turned and waved.

Olly almost swallowed his gum. "No way. Who do you talk to who's dead?"

"Well, like my parents. I talk to them a lot when I'm mad at my foster parents, especially now that we have to move."

"You're moving? When?" The taunts of the bullies grew louder in his head. The chill wasn't just the December wind. Had he just made one friend only to lose another?

Alex walked backward in front of the bikes. "Not till the end of term. I wish I was eighteen, so I wouldn't have to go with them."

Sid gave Olly a comforting look and shrugged. "That's six months away." And, with no hesitation, she asked Alex, "Who else do you talk to that's dead?"

Olly's head reeled. *How can she go on and on like that?*

Alex became solemn. "I talk to this little boy who died. I guess I imagine him looking down on me whenever it rains, so I look up into the rain and tell him how sorry I am. I kept him out too late one night last summer when I was babysitting him."

Olly's chin dropped. "What happened?" He looked at Sid, struck speechless but for entirely different reasons.

"I was babysitting him for the afternoon. We went to the park, but it started to, like, rain really hard, so I took him to a movie." She tucked in her chin and scuffed her heel in the dirt. "It was too early to take him home after the first movie, so we had hot dogs and stayed for the next one. It was still pouring when we got out, and it was really late when I got him home. His dad was, like, furious because he still had to drive him to Victoria to his mother's that night."

Images flashed through Olly's mind. *Boy. Rain. August. Highway. Malahat.* Could it be?

Sid was talking. "That's not fair. Couldn't he see it was raining?"

Alex kicked at nothing on the trail. "Yes, but I shouldn't have stayed for the second feature."

Gooseflesh crept up Olly's arms. Alex—his strong, mature

protector that no one messed with—looked like she was going to cry.

Sid just wouldn't let up. "How did he die?"

Olly did not want to hear any more about death and dying, but Alex seized the moment to let it all out in a torrent of tears.

"They were in a terrible car crash." She sobbed. "Teddy died… and his dad was in the hospital for a long time. I don't think he can work anymore. And it's all my fault."

"Teddy?" PJ *had* to be Teddy. Olly was going to be sick. He dropped his bike and ducked into the bushes. His head spun and his stomach convulsed—no stopping his lunch from spewing across the ground. He hung his head, bracing himself with his hands on his knees.

He could only catch the occasional word as Sid connected the dots for Alex. Storm… Olly saw… accident… teddy bear… pajamas…imaginary friend now.

When Olly felt Alex place her hand on his back, he wanted to die. He gagged again.

"I knew there was something special about you, Olly. I think it's superlative you have this cosmic gift." She kept stroking his back. "When I talk to Teddy, I don't have any sense of connection like you do though. Would you tell PJ, I mean Teddy, how sorry I am?" she sputtered. "How terrible I feel? I have nightmares. Is he mad at me like his dad?"

The taste of bile made Olly spit. He turned. Tears streamed down Alex's cheeks, leaving black trails under her eyes. And there stood PJ—Teddy—reaching for her hand.

The setting sun broke through the clouds and filtered a golden glow through the trees.

"He's smiling at you right now."

* * *

BY APRIL, Olly had come to terms with PJ's new name. The winter hadn't exactly flown by, but Alex and Sid had made it bearable. Spring on the island was now in full bloom. He sat beside his bike at the duck pond, scattering seeds to the ducks as they paddled through pink reflections of cherry blossoms, their beaks clattering like castanets.

He snickered and glanced at Teddy sitting on the grass in front of him, never speaking unless Olly spoke to him first. "Look at that one, Teddy. He's got a leech by his eye."

Ew, that's gross. Can you pick it off?

"No way. I can't catch a duck."

A voice startled him from behind. "Hey, weirdo. Who are you talking to? The fairies? You hear voices in your head? Ooooo."

Olly stiffened. He turned and saw Cole Thomas swaggering toward him with Alex in tow. *What did she see in him anyway? Just because he's a senior, I bet.* He strutted like a rooster around girls, but pretended like he couldn't care less. Nothin' but a big jock.

Alex scowled and crouched down to take some seeds from Olly's bag. "Shut up, Cole. You can be such an asshole sometimes. Olly's my friend." She threw the seeds across the water.

"Are you nuts? What do you want to be friends with this little creep for?"

Alex tossed her head. "Because he gets bullied by people like you, so apologize already."

"Get real." Cole flicked his chin at her before leaving.

Olly scrunched up his face until his eyebrows hurt. This wasn't the first time Cole had picked on him. Now Alex knew. *Just dump him—he's such a jerk.*

She sat on the bench beside him, tossing seeds on the water. "I *should* dump him, shouldn't I?"

Olly's eyes grew wide, his arm frozen mid-throw. "I didn't say anything. Did I?"

Alex shoulder-bumped him. "No, but you were thinking it."

FIVE

"APRIL SHOWERS BRING MAY FLOWERS, Mom said." Sid crouched beside her mother's headstone and chucked the dead stems over her head.

Olly passed her a handful of fresh flowers and sat on the cool grass beside her, hugging his knees. "Do you think she likes these flowers?"

"I know she liked them when she was alive. She grew them in our garden, but I can't take them from there in case Cruella sees me."

"Did your mom know Cruella?"

"No. But my dad knew her from the gym."

"Do you think they, you know, knew each other, like, really good?"

"I'm pretty sure. She even came to Mom's funeral."

Olly jumped up. "I got an idea. You should introduce them."

"What?"

"You know, the way we talk to them. Like I talk to Teddy." He looked over at Teddy, who was playing on a flat gravestone. "We'll help you. Right, Teddy?"

Teddy dragged his bear over and looked up at Olly for his cue.

Sid nodded. "Right." She positioned Olly on one side of the grave with herself on the other. She looked toward the foot of the grave.

"Okay, Cruella, you stand there so Mom can get a good look at you." She glanced at Olly. "I don't suppose you can see her there, can you?"

He shook his head vigorously. "Uh-uh, she's all yours."

Sid shrugged and addressed her mother's headstone. "Mom, this is Cruella, my wicked stepmother." She stuck her chubby forefinger at her stepmother. "Uh-uh. You don't get to speak."

She looked at the headstone. "Mom, did you know that Cruella went to the same gym as Dad? Yeah. And did you see her at your funeral? She's got some balls, right?" She looked at Olly for confirmation.

Olly grinned. "Yeah, some balls." He reached toward the headstone and pretended to shake hands. "Nice to see you again, Mrs. Wheeler. We brought you some flowers from my Aunt Lila's garden. Sid says they're your favorite."

Sid was really getting into her role. "You remember my friend Olly, and that little guy?" She pointed at the ground beside Olly. "Teddy is Olly's dead friend. Maybe you've met him. He's only four."

Olly looked at Teddy. "Wave at the nice lady." Teddy waved.

A voice startled Olly, making even Sid and Teddy jump. "So that's where my flowers are disappearing to."

Olly wheeled around. "Aunt Lila. What are you doing here?"

"I could ask you the same question."

"We're just visiting Sid's mother."

"Well, I'm visiting your Uncle Arthur, but I didn't bring him any flowers because his favorites were all gone." She pointed to the vase in front of Mrs. Wheeler's headstone.

Sid reached down and yanked them out of the water. "I'm sorry, Mrs. Forrester. Here. Take them to Uncle Arthur."

Aunt Lila chuckled. "It's all right, Sidney. I'm sure he will understand." She turned to walk back to her car. "We'll see you two back at home for supper, Olly."

Sid looked confused. "Did she just invite me for supper at your place?"

Olly had a sinking feeling in the pit of his stomach. "I don't think so. I think she caught me talking to Teddy again."

* * *

THE BACK DOOR squeaked a bit when Olly got home from the graveyard. He winced. Aunt Lila could be waiting to grill him about Teddy. He hesitated, then snuck upstairs. Her voice floated from the kitchen just as his mom opened the front door. "Lauren, I want to talk to you before Olly gets home."

Olly heard a heavy sigh. "All right. What has he done?"

He sat on the top step and listened.

"Apart from taking flowers from my garden, it's his acting out. I went to Arthur's grave today, and he was there with his little friend Sidney at her mother's grave."

"He took your flowers to the cemetery for Sidney's mother's grave?"

"Yes, but—"

"That was sweet of him, but Olly should have asked, I know. I'll have to speak to him about taking things without asking."

"You're not listening. That's not the worrying thing. He's still talking at inappropriate times and places."

"You mean to that teddy bear?"

"Yes, but it's also the whole playacting thing he does."

"What was he doing?"

"He and Sidney were acting out some conversation with her mother and someone who, they pretended, stood at the foot of the grave. Olly was standing on one side of the grave, and he was talking to 'Teddy,' who was supposedly on the ground beside him. But here's the thing: he didn't have that teddy bear with him."

"Oh, Lila, I think you're making too much of this. Children playact with imaginary friends all the time."

"Well, what about the call you got from his teacher? He's doing this in class, not just when he's by himself, but when the other kids can see him. Lauren, he's being bullied because of this."

"I spoke to him about that. Sidney does the same thing, and apparently there was an older student who stuck up for him. He really doesn't seem upset about all this. What do you expect me to do?"

"It all started when you moved in here. Did he have imaginary friends when you were with Curtis?"

"Well, he would playact with action figures and trucks and planes, but that's perfectly normal."

"But they weren't imaginary, Lauren. That's the thing. Listen, I have a friend, Christine Hunter, who is a retired psychologist. She still sees some patients from home. Why don't you have her talk to Oliver just to see if there is any underlying trauma he's trying to work out?"

"You really think Olly has a problem?"

"I don't know. But wouldn't it be better to find out?"

Olly tiptoed down the stairs and out the back door, only to turn around and stomp back in.

* * *

THAT NIGHT, Olly couldn't sleep. Moonlight streaming through the window lit up his room. He sat up in bed and smacked Teddy with Brad's bear. "Wake up."

Teddy rubbed his eyes. *What?*

"Aunt Lila talked Mom into having my head examined."

What for?

"She thinks I'm nuts 'cause I talk to you."

That's crazy.

Olly's mouth fell open. "That was stellar." He fell back and jammed the bear's head into his mouth to muffle his laugh. Teddy rolled around on the bed, howling.

"Shut up, Teddy. You want to wake up the whole house?"

Aw. They can't hear me. I can laugh loud enough to wake the dead.

That was too much. Olly laughed into his pillow till his sides hurt. All this stifled laughing was tiring. He rolled over and yawned. "You took the words right out of my head."

* * *

BUT IN THE MORNING, Olly awoke uneasy about what Aunt Lila had talked his mom into. He called Sid first. She agreed that Alex would know what to do. The sun was warm on his face as he biked over to Alex's house.

Alex opened the door and smiled. "Hey. What's up?"

In a loud whisper, he said, "I need to talk to you and Sid about something."

Alex retrieved her bike from the backyard, and they sped off to the duck pond to meet Sid, who pulled Olly down onto the bench by the sleeve. "What did your aunt say about the cemetery?"

"She thinks I'm nuts." Olly scowled.

Alex held up her hands. "Whoa! Start at the beginning. What happened at the cemetery?"

Sid's and Olly's exclamations collided in mid-air until Alex zipped her lips at them. "Hold on. You conjured up Cruella de Vil to be part of this?"

Olly slapped his forehead. "No, silly, that's just what Sid calls her stepmother. We wanted to introduce her to Sid's mom."

Sid's head bobbed. "Right, because I figure my dad and her were foolin' around before mom died. And I wanted to see her squirm."

"Okay, okay. So the gang was all there, and I'm guessing your aunt caught you."

"Yeah. She heard me talking to Teddy."

"So now she's got your mom, like, all worried?"

"Right. What am I going to do? She's going to send me to some doctor!" Olly's eyes filled with tears.

Sid rolled her eyes. "This is not good. They sent my cousin to a shrink because he was acting up in school and wouldn't listen. They gave him some medicine that made him all dopey and stuff."

Alex shook her head and placed her hand on Olly's back. "This is not the same at all, Sid. Your cousin was probably hyperactive. They probably put him on Ritalin."

Olly wiped his nose on his sleeve. "How do you know all this stuff?"

"There were kids in my last school who were climbing the walls. But once they were put on Ritalin, they calmed right down. They didn't like it, though, so they got a 'day off' once in a while. But, you have to be careful, Olly."

Olly didn't think he was squirrely, but he sure felt like climbing a tree and staying there. "What do you mean?"

"You're different from those kids. You're just talking to a dead boy. We have to figure out what you should say." Alex put her finger to her chin and looked at the sky.

Sid swung her feet around and sat cross-legged. "Would it help if Olly tells them I talk to my dead mom and Cruella when she's not there?"

"I dunno. Do you see your mom when she was sick and dying, or when she was healthy and pretty?"

"I guess when she was happy, like the picture in my room."

"That's not the same as Olly. He sees Teddy the way he died, in a car crash." Her eyes opened wide, and she jabbed her finger at him. "And you definitely can't tell her that."

Olly slid off the bench beside Teddy and flopped onto the grass, his whole body limp with despair. "I'm doomed."

* * *

SUDDENLY IT WAS JUNE, and two weeks before grad. The three friends were again on the same bench, only this time it was Alex who was inconsolable. Olly and Sid sat on either side of her, swinging their legs and listening to her snuffle. A lady and a little girl were feeding the ducks on the other side.

Olly punched his palm. *I hate him. Poor Alex—dumped.* "What did you want to go out with Cole for, anyway? He's just a big jock. You called him an asshole, even."

"I know. I thought he was going to ask me to the grad dance, but he's taking Georgia instead of me. Georgia! My best friend, and she didn't tell me."

Olly couldn't think of a thing to say, so he signaled with his eyes for Sid to say something. Lucky for him, she did.

"Georgia's a traitor. She was just pretending to be your friend. And I heard her say that you must be dumb to walk home with us little kids."

Alex stopped crying. "Did she really say that?"

"Yeah. And I saw her rubbing her tits on Cole's arm once." Sid crossed her arms and raised her eyebrows at Olly.

A vigorous nod from him confirmed it. "Yeah."

Alex honked into a tissue. "And now he's taking her to the grad dance."

"Well, at least you won't see them together, because you can't go. You're not a senior."

Sid frowned at him like he was an idiot, which he had to admit he was.

Alex's head shot up, and the wailing started again. "But I already bought my dress!"

SIX

IT WAS FRIDAY, June 27, the last day of school, and Olly had never been so miserable—not when his uncle had died, and not even when they'd left his dad. The plan was to invite Alex to the movie with him and Sid tonight, but she had gone to Connie's Café with Georgia instead of walking home with them. Second fiddle to Georgia the traitor. *What's up with that?*

Deflated, he and Sid had gone to the movie on their own. Afterwards, Sid's dad had picked her up, leaving Olly to ride his bike alone through the park. It was late... and dark. As he approached the black patches between lights, the trees bent toward him, rustling their leaves like chains.

The trees wailed, and an owl screeched. If he pedaled faster, maybe he wouldn't die. Tears ran back into his ears. Alex was moving to Campbell River tomorrow. *Didn't even say goodbye.* He closed his eyes for a moment to remember how she'd looked today: her ripped jeans, a T-shirt, and her favorite red scarf wrapped around her neck.

"Whee!" Alex leaped onto his handlebars, making him swerve and almost tip over.

Olly's fear vanished in an instant, and his heart soared. "Hey! You scared the crap out of me. Where'd you come from?"

"I knew you and Sid were going to the movie tonight, and I wanted to say goodbye. I got you good, didn't I?"

"That's for sure." Olly pedaled past his house and down the street to Alex's. Now that she was with him, the dark spots between the streetlights weren't so scary. Her long red scarf fluttered around his head.

Alex hopped off his handlebars and gave him a little peck on the cheek. "I'm going to miss my little buddy. You be cool in that interview with the psychologist, okay?"

Olly blushed. He'd never been kissed by a girl before, except for his mom and Aunt Lila. "Sure, Alex. I remember what you told me." He was so flustered he rode off without saying goodbye. He looked over his shoulder and shouted, "Goodbye!" but Alex had gone inside.

* * *

OLLY BOUNCED through the front door and headed for the stairs, the tingle of Alex's kiss still on his cheek.

His mom called after him from the kitchen. "Olly, dear, brush your teeth well after all that junk food."

"I will, Mom. Good night."

He brushed his teeth with exaggerated gusto, spat, and rinsed. He smiled at himself in the mirror, the warmth of his blush returning. *Wow! Alex is so cool.* But his reflected smile dissolved. *And now she's gone.*

He dragged his feet down the hall, pulling off his T-shirt as he walked into his room. His head popped out, and there was Alex... sitting on his bed, playing with Teddy.

"Hi," she said.

Olly yelped, frozen in his footsteps. "What are you doing here?"

Downstairs, his mother called, "Are you all right, Olly?"

40

"Uh… just stubbed my toe. I'm fine." But he wasn't. This was freaky.

Alex tiptoed to the door and listened.

Olly's head spun. For a second, he heard nothing. But then her voice popped into his head. *You should, like, close the door.*

"Yeah." Olly's mouth hung open. He closed it without letting it click. He forgot he was half-dressed and sat on the edge of the bed. "Are you dead, Alex?"

Again, her voice just came to him. *I don't think so. I just moved to Campbell River.*

Olly sighed heavily. "Whew, that's a relief. I thought maybe you got killed like Teddy." He cocked his head to one side. "If you're my new imaginary friend, you can help babysit him."

I guess.

Olly started taking off his jeans but then jerked them up again. "Hey, you can't be here when I'm getting into my pajamas."

How about I just turn around?

"Okay, but no peeking." Olly quickly changed and jumped into bed, pulling the covers up to his chin. "You can turn around."

Alex tucked Teddy in beside him and perched on the end of the bed.

You know what this means, don't you?

"What?"

I can go with you to see that shrink!

* * *

THE DREADED DAY arrived for Olly's scheduled meeting with Christine Hunter. He rubbed his sweaty palms on his jeans as the streets whizzed by.

Before they got out of the car, his mom gave him a big hug. "I think you'll like Christine. She's a good friend of your Aunt Lila's. She's just going to ask you a few questions about your imaginary friend, okay?"

"I guess." He was much more relaxed now that Alex would be

there, too. He climbed out of the car and walked up to the front door of the doctor's house behind his mom. The shrink greeted them with a smile. He glanced back at Alex with Teddy in tow. "Well, here we go."

Olly caught the quizzical look his mother gave Christine. *Oops. Busted.*

* * *

AN HOUR LATER, Olly emerged, smiling for his mom. She breathed a little sigh of relief. "How did it go?"

"Okay, I guess. She said you should go in."

As soon as the door closed behind her, Alex plunked herself down in the chair beside him. *You did good, Olly. I don't think she's going to give you the medicine that makes you dopey.* Teddy sat on her knee and nodded.

She giggled. *I thought it was funny when she asked if you were afraid of Teddy. And you made her promise not to tell your mom about him. Smart you.* Alex twirled the ends of her red scarf.

"Yeah. She would have freaked out if I'd told her about *you* being my imaginary friend *too*. And I've got to remember: Mom thinks you're an older boy who still lives on my street." Olly sighed. "I have to try 'thinking' my words when I talk to you. That's going to be hard, especially with Teddy."

Alex paced around the foyer. *But I can still, like, talk out loud, right? No one can hear me?*

"I guess not. I can only hear you in my head." Olly screwed up his nose. "Doctor Christine wants me to keep this journal. Like an experiment, she said, so I don't wave my arms around when we're talking. But no way I can write down everything I say to you guys."

Alex gazed out the front door. *Well, if this works, you won't get bullied anymore.*

"I hope not, because you won't be here—in person, I mean."

Olly snapped his finger to his lips the instant the door to Christine's office opened. *I'd better start this 'thinking' at you right now, Alex.*

SEVEN

IT HAD BEEN a year since Alex had moved away. Sid turned toward Olly and tapped the back of the bench. "You know, we've been sitting on this bench for two whole years. We should put a plaque here that says 'Sid Wheeler and Olly Frampton sat here since 2008.'"

Olly scoffed. "Don't most of those plaques say 'in memory of'?" He glanced at Alex, who sat on the edge of the pond while Teddy dangled his feet in the water.

Alex looked up at him. *It could say 'In Memory of Teddy Something and Alexis Young.'*

Surprised by her words, Olly spoke out loud. "Don't be stupid, Alex. We can't call him Teddy Something and besides, you're not dead."

Sid jumped up and put her hands on her hips. "Do you have to bring her everywhere we go? She spoils everything. She's been gone a year, so get over it already."

Before Olly could think of an answer—since, of course, there wasn't one—Sid jumped on her bike and rode off in a huff.

Olly half rose to follow her, but changed his mind. He looked at

Alex and Teddy with narrowed eyes. "Why can't you stay at home—out of my head? Stop causing trouble."

Alex twirled her scarf around her finger the way she always did when she teased him. *She's just mad because she knows you like me.*

"Shut up!" His cheeks grew hot.

Ducks startled and fluttered a few feet away, and a woman passing by gave him a wide berth. She yanked the hand of her little girl, who clutched a bag of birdseed to her chest.

Olly's heart sank. *I'll never be free of them if I can't even keep my mouth shut.*

He jumped on his bike, spraying cedar chips into the air, the little girl's words ringing in his ears. "Why did he yell at the ducks, Mommy?"

* * *

ANOTHER THREE TEMPESTUOUS years rolled by with Teddy and Alex dogging Olly, sometimes at the most inopportune moments. It had now been five years since Teddy had appeared in the back seat and become part of Olly's life—and four since Alex had broken his prepubescent heart and become his second imaginary friend.

Olly sat at his desk in his room, staring out the window, his pen poised over an empty page in his journal.

Since the day she had kissed him on the cheek and then moved to Campbell River—well, maybe even before that—he had been smitten. But sometimes she acted more like an older sister with her sage advice and teasing, and it wounded his fragile ego.

Why can't I imagine her liking me? It was infuriating. He looked at a blank page. *Should I record this?* A year ago, she had caught him kissing his pillow. He'd wanted to die. More pointedly, he'd wished *she* would die—and he'd told her so.

Olly waffled between extremes of emotion whenever he thought of Alex.

Only the day before, she'd pretended to blow out the thirteen candles on his birthday cake before he could. "Don't you dare!" he'd yelled at her, and everybody had stopped singing, including his dad, who had come up from Victoria especially for the occasion.

Sid, as always, had jumped to his rescue. She'd puffed out her cheeks, laughed, and winked at him. "I wasn't really going to blow them out, Olly. Honest."

Olly still wasn't speaking to Alex. He would bike over to the gas station and buy some junk with his birthday money. It was only two weeks before school started again, so he wouldn't spend much. His mom had made him promise to buy some new runners.

The familiar smell of gas as he passed the pumps made him think of the crash, Teddy, and inevitably Alex. *Darn.* He leaned his bike against the tire rack out front. Alex perched on top.

"I'm not talking to you."

Alex shrugged, but someone at the pumps said, "Well, if it isn't the nutjob who talks to the fairies."

Olly cringed. Every year around his birthday, that was the one rotten thing that happened: Cole came back to town after working away all summer.

Olly tried to ignore him and dash into the store, but there was no escape. Cole was right behind him. Olly grabbed a bag of chips and a couple of chocolate bars and dropped them on the counter.

Alex put her thumbs in her ears and stuck her tongue out at Cole. *Just ignore him, Olly. He's still an asshole. Did you see Georgia in the car?*

Yeah, Olly had seen her. All he wanted to do was pay for his stuff and get out of there.

Too late. Georgia sauntered in. "Hey, squirt. Didn't you used to be Alex's little gopher? She was such a loser." She leaned on Cole's arm and cracked her gum.

That was it. Olly lashed out. "Alex is—was—my friend. A better friend than you ever were to her. I'd rather be friends with fairies than that asshole." He poked a finger in Cole's direction and charged out the door without his change, heat rising in his neck.

Cole was on his tail like a mongoose. He grabbed Olly by the back of his shirt and shoved him to the ground. "Who do you think you're calling an asshole? You little cretin."

Georgia snorted. "Some friend. Does she call you and write you letters? Is she even in Campbell River?" She scoffed at Olly, stuck her nose in the air, and turned on her heel.

Cole smacked the back of her head as she got in the car.

"Ow. What was that for?"

"Just shut up."

Looking up at Alex, Olly struggled to his feet and rubbed his knee. *Is that true? Didn't you move there with your foster parents?*

She scowled after Cole's car as it pulled away from the pumps. *That's what I thought.*

Olly snuffled, his bike zigzagging into the empty street with Alex on his handlebars. "I don't hate the *real* you, you know. It's just *this* you that drives me crazy."

* * *

OLIVER AWOKE IN A BAD MOOD. Being fourteen was the shits. Another year, another birthday disaster to live down. And this time Sid hadn't been there to rescue him. Why did he always seem to conjure up these stupid scenarios that could only lead to something weird. This year he had tackled Brad around the ankles thinking Teddy had fallen off Alex's shoulders. What's up with that? The awkward silence and Brad's condescension had completed Oliver's humiliation, and the party had fizzled like a dead balloon.

He pulled the sheet over his head when his mother poked her head in the door.

"Hurry up, Olly. You don't want to be late for your first day of grade nine."

He gritted his teeth. "Mom, could you stop calling me Olly, please? It sounds so babyish."

She gazed at him and wrinkled her brow. "Hmm. I'll try to remember that, Olly... uh, Oliver." She smiled and headed downstairs. "Better get up, dear."

Alex sat on the end of his bed, playing pat-a-cake with Teddy.

"And I'm not taking you two with me this year," Oliver whispered. "You hear me? I don't need you making me look like an idiot."

Oliver schlepped out of bed and headed for the bathroom. He was too old for imaginary friends and relentless torment, with Alex annoying him and Teddy pestering him to find his 'mommy.' Why couldn't Alex just be a good babysitter for Teddy? The only real friend he could count on was Sid.

He mumbled as he lifted the toilet lid. "I wish I could get rid of you for good."

Alex's voice came from the shower. *That's just what I was thinking.*

"Geez, Alex. A little privacy here. Sometimes I wish you were dead." Oliver clamped his hands over his genitals.

Maybe I already am, like Teddy. But that doesn't mean I'll go away for sure, does it?

"Get out of here! Get out of my head!"

There was a rap at the door. "Olly, are you all right?"

"Yes, Mom. Just thinking out loud. I'll be right down."

"Well, try to curb that habit at school. Remember what Dr. Christine told you about stress?"

* * *

TIME DIDN'T EXACTLY FLY by for Oliver. The first two years of high school were almost as miserable as elementary school. Sorting out the pecking order was stressful and, of course, with stress came Alex and Teddy. But he'd learned a trick. If he inadvertently blurted something stupid out of context, he would quickly open a book—any book—and "check his notes for accuracy." Then he would nod, slam it shut, and close his eyes. It worked every time.

Life became easier in Grade Eleven. He had mastered silent communication with Alex and Teddy, if he even thought of them at all. And on one of his annual visits to Christine Hunter, she suggested another strategy to control his gesturing if they appeared to him spontaneously during times of elevated stress: he could point at the intruder in his mind with his finger or a pen, then glance thoughtfully at the ceiling. No one would be the wiser. He added that to his arsenal of coping techniques.

Today, Olly's history teacher, Mr. Powell, leaned against his desk with an armload of papers. "Oliver Frampton."

This was it. His first major paper. He wiped his sweaty palms on his thighs and walked up to receive it.

"This is a fine essay, Oliver. 'Interviewing' Alexander the Great in the first person was a brilliant idea. It has depth and captures a believable essence of his psyche. Well done. A-plus."

When Mr. Powell shook his hand, Oliver couldn't believe it. He had been toying with the idea of doing a series of articles for the high-school newspaper, *The Hub*, on historical figures from their courses. This one had been a trial run. Alexander the Great may not have had those thoughts or made those statements, but his interview responses were consistent with the outcome in history.

When he'd suggested the idea to Sid, she'd been his biggest cheerleader. *"Olly, go for it. I know this will be a hit. What are you waiting for? Get writing!"*

At the end of classes, she caught him in the hall, gave him a big hug, and shook him by the shoulders. "What did I tell you? A-plus, not bad. You *are* going to submit it to *The Hub*?"

"Yeah, I guess." He set her at arm's length by the waist.

He blushed a little when other students high-fived him as they passed. Hearing "way to go, man" was a new sensation for him.

He swung his backpack over his shoulder. "You want to stop for coffee at Connie's? I want to run an idea by you."

Sid bobbed her eyebrows. "I'm intrigued."

She passed him in her VW beater and, as usual, ordered for both of them before he had even parked his bike.

He slid into the booth across from her. "Thanks. You know I always let you win, so you'll buy." He held his cup in both hands and blew across it.

"I know. What's your next brilliant idea?"

"I don't know if it's even ethical, but I was thinking of making up a life story for Teddy. Odd that we never knew his last name." He scowled for a second. "And I could do an essay on Alex too, but with a future I design for her instead of a past. It's her future that is the unknown. I think it would be therapeutic for me to get them out of my head and on paper. Those old journals Christine got me to write will be useful. I'm glad you made me keep them. What do you think?"

Alex popped up on the seat beside him. *I think it's a radical idea. Make me super rich or something really cool.*

"No way, Alex. You'll have no input."

Sid raised her eyebrows and pointed her spoon at the space beside Oliver. "She got her two cents' worth in already, eh?"

Oliver rocked his head with a resigned grin.

"Well, if I can render my opinion…" Sid stared into nothing. "I think it would be very good for you, but I think you'd have to alter the names and details the way they do in movies to avoid libel suits. Because you never know. Alex may surface in some exotic place with a plausible explanation for not keeping in touch."

"Good point. I wouldn't even be questioning where Alex is now if Georgia hadn't brought it up. It's a cinch this Alex doesn't know where she is." He puffed out his cheeks and exhaled. "What am I saying? She doesn't know because *I* don't know."

"That's true. But I want you to continue with these historical figures from our courses this term. Next year, when you graduate, you can tackle your Teddy and Alex stories. By then, they'll already know you in journalistic circles, I guarantee it."

"You guarantee it, do you?"

"Yes. You could even enter these essays into writing contests. There's some money in it. I sure would if I had your talent."

"You are so competitive." He leaned back and put his arm on the back of the booth. "Like, you always have to be ahead of me. What's with that?"

Sid waggled her head and gave him a little eye roll. "I just like the idea of you chasing me."

"What do you mean? I don't need to catch you. We've been

joined at the hip since grade three." He took a sip. Thoughts began churning.

Alex leaned over from the booth behind him. *Hello? Is anyone home? You are so clueless, Olly. She wants to cut your grass.*

Oliver's eyes bulged. "Is that true?"

Sid sipped her coffee. "Is what true?"

"Do you want to cut my grass?"

Sid snorted coffee out of her nose and choked. Oliver shook with stifled laughter and handed her a serviette.

"Where the hell did you get that from? Alex?"

"My aunt uses that phrase. I guess I channeled it through Alex. Are you okay?"

Sid blew her nose. "Sure. So do I get the job?"

"What job?"

Her mouth dropped open. "Cutting your damn grass, you idiot!"

"Oh, yeah. It's been overgrown for a couple of years now." He reached across the table, squeezed her hand, and chuckled. Sometimes Alex made him finally see things that had been percolating in his mind for a long, long time.

* * *

A YEAR LATER, still wearing his tux from the night before, Oliver basked in the glow of the morning sun as he biked home from Sid's place. He leaned his bike against the garage and entered the house by the side door. His mother glanced at him between bites of her scrambled eggs.

"I hope you didn't lose the tie and cummerbund."

Oliver fished them out of his pocket. "Right here, Mom."

"Good. You can return them this afternoon so we don't get charged extra."

"Sure. What did you think of the ceremony?"

"It was lovely. And Sidney looked so beautiful in her gown."

"I know Sid appreciated your commenting on it—she thinks highly of you."

"Well, she's had a hard time of it with that stepmother of hers."

Oliver nodded. "I'm sure that old beater her father bought her last year was meant to ease his conscience. I'm going to run upstairs and change out of this getup. Will you be here for a bit? I'd like to talk."

"I'll be here."

Oliver bounded up the steps two at a time and stripped out of his tuxedo. He'd gotten used to Alex being in the same room when he was changing, but he drew the line at the bathroom door, where he made sure something else entirely occupied his mind.

Back in the kitchen, he poured himself a coffee and spun a chair around to straddle it. He placed a letter in front of his mother and rested his chin on his arms.

She snatched it from the table, mumbling every other word as she read. "You got the courses you wanted. Oh, Olly, this is just wonderful. Congratulations."

"Thanks, Mom. I've been thinking of getting a part-time job to help pay for this, but—"

"No. I told you. You are to concentrate on your studies. I've planned for your education, and your dad has contributed as well, so no job unless the paper asks you for an article." She poked her index finger in the air. "And it has to be within the scope of your studies."

"All right, but you know Sidney has to work to maintain her apartment, and I feel bad that I have this allowance."

"I know. Sidney's had it rough. I want you to help her out whenever you can."

"I do, Mom."

"She's been a good friend to you all these years."

"Yes." Oliver sighed and looked askance at his mom. "But we've been more than friends for a long time now—you know that. It's funny. Who would have thought I'd wind up with a girl I met in grade three?" They both laughed. But Alex didn't. The tables were turned now that Oliver was three years older than the fifteen-year-old Alex sitting on the edge of the counter swinging her legs and pouting. Now she could moon over him for a change, after all those years he'd crushed on her. He smirked to himself. *Serves her right.*

His mother poured them each another cup. "Remember when we kept journals—you about PJ and me about you?"

It occurred to Oliver that his mother didn't know who PJ was—that he was real and had a name. She still thought of him as an imaginary friend that Oliver had conceived to help him cope with his homesickness when they first left Victoria. Luckily, his coping skills had managed to conceal Teddy's, and Alex's, lingering presence over the years.

"Uh, yes. That was a useful experiment, notwithstanding the time Cole stole it and read it to the other jocks."

"Wasn't it Sidney who got it back for you?"

Oliver turned the chair around and slouched on it. "Yes. She broke into his locker and stole it back, then proceeded to spread his shorts on the bushes outside."

"Did she really? For heaven's sake, I didn't hear that. That boy was so incorrigible. Whatever happened to him?"

"Oh, he's still around. I think he works at the junkyard way out on Jingle Pot Road. And he used to work up in Campbell River during summer break."

"A sad case." His mother shook her head. "Who knows what kind of home life he had growing up?" She stared out the window with the coffeepot poised over his mug for a few seconds. "Did you keep those journals?"

"Yes. And I may have found a use for them in a project I'm planning. Luckily, Sid made me pack them away when I finally had them —I mean PJ—under control."

Oliver avoided eye contact with his mother. Sometimes he wondered who he was protecting with this deception.

EIGHT

OLIVER UNLOCKED his bike and gazed at the gray sky. The smell of wet concrete mingled with the sweet aroma of jasmine that climbed the arbor above the bike rack. Straddling his bike, he texted Sid; he was leaving the university for the library. He swung into the street well behind the traffic, knowing the hill would be slick from the steady rain.

Professor Keegan had assigned a major end-of-term project on investigative journalism in crime reporting. It made Oliver keen to dive into the local and national newspaper archives. His first task was to search for articles on crimes for which there was no follow-up in the press. If that didn't yield results, he could always approach the police.

The wind was cool on his face as he coasted down the hill. He hopped off his bike as he approached the forty-foot tuning fork in Diana Krall Plaza. Oliver grinned at John, who was sitting in an alcove by the library entrance, the only dry spot in the plaza.

"Hey, John. Still redecorating your suite at the Ritz, are they?"

"Yup. And I ain't payin' 'em one red cent until they're done, the buggers."

"Damn straight." Oliver set the kickstand on his bike and palmed John a buck. "Keep an eye on it for me, John?"

"You got it, Olly."

Oliver liked John. Years ago, John had told him his name was actually John Francis Doe. He was confident the "John Doe" part was his name, but he wasn't sure where the "Francis" part had come from. They kept up the pretense of John being temporarily inconvenienced out of his lodgings. He might be homeless, but he had his pride.

Inside, Oliver shook the rain off his coat, greeted the librarian with a nod, and headed for the computer terminals. As he scrolled through the indices, the rush of excitement made him flex his fingers and take a deep breath. *Now... to challenge my investigative skills.*

As the hours rolled by, he noted articles on crimes in which the perpetrators had been unknown at the time of reporting or, if there had been an arrest, the name of the accused. He would check the court records on those before calling the local RCMP detachment. This was good. He rubbed his palms together.

He had three excellent prospects: a home invasion with two victims—suspect never caught—a suspicious drowning, and a body found in an alley. Had they interviewed the others in the alley? Shoddy investigating if they hadn't.

The next issue of the Observer he scrolled through was dated July fifth, just six weeks before his ninth birthday. And below the fold on the front page, he saw her. His heart leaped from his chest.

"Alex!" He froze, his fingers poised above the keyboard.

"Shush." An elderly gentleman scowled over his small round glasses.

Alex appeared from between the stacks. *What?*

A chill ran down his spine. His outburst erased all his years of discipline, and he was back to square one: verbalizing with her.

"This article is all about you." Oliver motioned her closer so he wouldn't have to shout. "It says you disappeared under suspicious circumstances."

The gentleman stood and gave Oliver a withering glare. "Would you kindly keep your voice down? I don't know to whom you think you're speaking, but it certainly isn't me. I didn't disappear under suspicious circumstances."

Oliver cringed with embarrassment. "I'm so sorry." He pointed at the screen and slumped in his chair.

Alex leaned over his shoulder. *What does it say?*

Oliver tried to whisper from the side of his mouth. "Read for yourself."

The essence of the article was that Alexis Young had disappeared on the last day of school. She'd been last seen at Connie's Café after leaving Monteith Regional High School at around three thirty. Police were interviewing all her known friends, fellow students, teachers, and her unnamed foster parents. They found no evidence that she had planned to leave home, and none of her personal possessions were missing.

Oliver's hands trembled as he scrolled through the next ten issues, searching for follow-up articles. He found only one small item that reported "no new leads into her disappearance." Oliver ordered hard copies of the two articles, then signed out. He grabbed his backpack and hustled out into a threatening rain. *Shit.*

He almost neglected to acknowledge John as he pulled his collar up to his ears.

All discipline gone; the words leaped from his mouth. "Alex, I want to have a long talk with you when we get home."

You know I don't know anything.

"Semantics. Then I'll pick my brain through you."

Can I ride on the back of your bike?

"No. Find your own way home." Oliver wasn't usually so unfeeling with Alex—he had resigned himself to her presence and ignored her when he didn't want to be disturbed—but this was different. This new knowledge went against everything he'd thought was true about her disappearance. But what had he known about the news when he was eight going on nine? Nothing.

John gave him an understanding nod. It had been years since he'd heard Oliver talking to himself. No judgement.

* * *

OLIVER RUSHED in the back door and bounded up the stairs two at a time.

"Olly, is that you?" Aunt Lila called from the kitchen.

He looked over his shoulder. "Yes. I need to speak to Mom as soon as she gets here."

"I'll tell her."

In his room, Oliver whipped his laptop out of his backpack and booted up. He paced, ignoring Alex, who sat cross-legged on the end of his bed in her extreme jeans (still out at the knees), her white T-shirt, and her long red scarf: the same clothes she'd worn on that last day of school and for twelve years since.

What happened to me, Olly?

"I don't know. I'm going to ask Mom about it first, so just chill and let me think." He continued to pace.

It wasn't long before he heard his aunt's voice, followed by his mother's footfalls on the stairs and a tap at the door.

"You wanted to see me?"

"Come in, Mom."

"What's going on?" She sat and patted the bed beside her.

Olly motioned for Alex to move over before he sat. He wished his mother hadn't seen that. It had been a long time since he'd acknowledged an imaginary friend in her presence.

"I was down at the library, doing research into old crimes for an assignment, when I came across an article about the disappearance of Alexis Young. It was always my understanding that she moved with her foster family to Campbell River. But this article said her disappearance was suspicious. And I couldn't find any further news except that the police had suspended the search for her. Do you remember anything about that?"

"Oh my gosh, Oliver. That was—what? Twelve years ago? I

remember hearing that she was unhappy that they were moving, so the police thought she was a runaway. They searched the park and logging roads but found nothing. It made parents jittery that summer, because Alexis was an excellent student and had big plans for university. Don't you remember hearing anything at school?"

Oliver couldn't sit still. He began pacing again. "I was in grade three, Mom—a different school. I didn't hear a thing."

"Why are you so upset? Did you know this girl?"

Well, there it was—the moment of truth. Oliver flopped onto the bed. "Yes, I knew her. On my first day of school here, she was kind to me when I was bullied. We became friends and frequently walked home together. She lived just two blocks down from here." Oliver sighed. "I had a terrible crush on her that year, and when she didn't walk home with me on that last day, I was heartbroken. That night she became my second imaginary friend, and she's been hanging around ever since."

His mother patted his knee. "I always thought it was another boy."

Oliver sat up. "You knew?"

"I suspected. And it's fine. You seemed all right with it."

He exhaled as the relief spread through his shoulders. "You know, thanks to Christine, I adopted some effective coping skills and got better at ignoring Alex and Teddy over the years. I seldom get animated or verbal anymore, but today at the library, I freaked out this guy to where he asked me to cease and desist. Awkward."

"Teddy? I thought you called him PJ?"

Oliver shook his head. "That's a whole other story, Mom."

Teddy looked up when he heard his name. *Did you find Mommy at the lib'ary too, Olly?*

Oliver shook his head in Teddy's direction.

His mother rose when Brad bellowed from the foot of the stairs. "Dinner's ready."

"Oliver, we can talk more about this later, all right?"

"Sure." He held up a hand to silence Alex and texted Sidney with clammy hands.

Oliver: Tim's @7?
Sidney: Sup?
Oliver: Alex.
Sidney: K.

Alex sat on the end of his bed, hugging her knees. *You're going to meet her, aren't you?*

Oliver still enjoyed messing with her head. *Of course. And Alex, I'd appreciate it if you didn't come along.*

Fat chance. You're going to talk about me behind my back.

* * *

WHEN OLIVER TURNED into the parking lot at Tim Hortons, it was still drizzling, which made his mood even more miserable. Sid's beater was already there. He jammed his bike into the rack and locked it.

Two coffees steamed on the table in front of Sid. *That's my girl.*

He shook the wet off his jacket and slid in across from her. "Thanks."

"No sweat. What's this about Alex?"

"You will not believe this."

"Try me."

Oliver popped the lid and took a cautious sip. "You know that assignment I'm researching?"

Sid cocked her head to one side.

"I came across reports of several suspicious deaths with little or no follow-up. So I was on a roll, right?"

She made a "give me more" gesture with both hands.

"Then, in a 2009 issue—early July—I found this article about the 'disappearance of fifteen-year-old Alexis Young.'" He shoved the hard copy of the article in front of her. "And there she was, just as I remember her—just as I've seen her for the last twelve years. That's her school picture. That's not what she wore to school that day. I'm telling you, Sid, I just about puked."

Her eyes grew wide. "No duh." She snatched the sheet and held her hand up like a crossing guard.

Oliver drummed his fingers around his mug and waited.

When she'd finished, she exhaled and shook her head. "Incredible." She ran her fingers over the print.

Oliver grabbed her hands and brought them to his lips.

"She disappeared around four o'clock on her way home from school on that last day." Oliver released her hands and beat his temples with his knuckles. "She jumped onto my handlebars that same day, only it was later, about nine thirty. You remember. It was after the movie. Your dad picked you up, but I had my bike." He looked at Sid through glazed eyes. "Could she have died then, like Teddy? Teddy appeared in the car with me when he died. But where was Alex between four and nine thirty?"

Sid pried open his fists. "What's the saying? Think horses, not zebras. She disappeared, Olly. That's all we know."

Oliver warmed at the diminutive she seldom used. "I'll cling to that thought." Oliver sighed. "Since her foster parents didn't raise the alarm until the next day, it wasn't until Sunday, after grad, that the RCMP started contacting her friends. They seemed to accept the runaway theory a little too quickly. If she'd been planning to run away, she would have teased us with that idea just to see our reaction."

"Absolutely. What do *you* remember about that night after we left the movie?"

"I remember thinking how bummed out she was about moving to Campbell River and how much I'd miss her. It was cloudy that night, so no moon, which had me nervous to begin with, and that was when she scared the shit out of me by jumping on my bike. She said she just wanted to say goodbye. When I dropped her at her house, she kissed my cheek."

"That sounds like delusional thinking, Olly."

"Of course it was. I was eight. It wasn't until I got home and found her in my room that I realized she had become my imaginary friend. Shit. I always thought she just moved away." He held his head and closed his eyes. "I must have been one of the last people to see her."

"Did the police talk to you at the time?"

"If I had been, I would have told you, and they might have found her. No. I wasn't one of her *real* friends. But we always talked on the way home."

Alex leaned over from the booth behind Oliver and startled him. *Yeah. I told you stuff I never shared with my besties. They could turn on you like a rattlesnake.*

"Dammit, Alex. Don't sneak up on me like that."

Sidney rolled her eyes. "I'll bet she's sticking out her tongue at me right now, isn't she?"

"Don't encourage her, Sid."

"Well, don't talk to her, then. You've lost your discipline." Sid took a sip. "I take it you're going to follow up on her disappearance for your assignment?"

"Hell, no. It's taken years to get my connection to her and Teddy under control. If I pursue this, all my efforts will be for nothing."

"You're kidding, right? You probably knew her better than anyone else. From what you've told me, you were her confidant, not likely ever to repeat her innermost thoughts."

"Because I didn't have any friends to tell them to, right?" Oliver stuck out his chin in defiance.

"Well… yeah, except me. You didn't exactly attract friends." Sid imitated the way Oliver used to act when he argued with some invisible entity. "And I stopped talking to my dead mom when I was ten."

"Okay, okay. I get your point." Oliver shivered all over. "But that's exactly why I don't want to look into this. I've already regressed to speaking to them out loud again."

"Look at this from a different angle. What if you need to do this to get her out of your head? I mean, come on. You've been trying to get rid of her for years, and that little pest Teddy as well."

Alex tapped Oliver on the shoulder. *What if she's got it figured? Like, if you find me, maybe I'll go away and I won't interfere with your relationship anymore. You know I hate her, right? And maybe I'll take Teddy home too.*

Oliver screwed up his face, pointed over his shoulder, and nodded.

Sid leaned back and laughed. "She agrees with me for once. I'm so glad you put the words into her mouth."

* * *

THAT NIGHT, Oliver couldn't sleep. "I do not want to do this. I've got to focus on these other unresolved stories, not yours. Look at me. I'm talking out loud to you again."

Alex spun around and around in his computer chair, annoying him. Odd, it didn't squeak when *she* did that. Had he never noticed that before? He scoffed. *You idiot, the chair isn't spinning for her—it never did.* He waved his arms in exasperation.

"Do you realize how many years it's taken to get over being that jerky, gesturing geek who argued with himself? You and Teddy caused me a lot of grief."

It wasn't that bad in the beginning, when we were just friends walking home from school.

"Why *did* you befriend me, Alex? I mean, I was eight, and you were fifteen."

I guess I didn't like the way they treated you when Teddy was around. It was bullying. But I didn't understand what was, like, going on in your head until I—Alex made air quotes—*disappeared.*

Oliver sat up and punched his pillow behind his back. "And I didn't want that friendship to end. You broke my little heart when you left, Alex. I guess that was the trauma that triggered it, just like Teddy's accident."

Teddy perked up at the mention of his name. *Did I follow you to school, Olly?* He was resting his chin in his hands at the foot of the bed, his pajamas and teddy bear just as wet and muddy as the night of the accident.

"Yes, you did, Teddy, for a long time. But you're happy to stay home and play with these old toys now, right?" The Lego kit had long since found themselves at the thrift store, but Oliver could still visualize them for Teddy's amusement. Teddy held up a Lego fire-fighter, making Oliver smile and nod.

Sure, Olly. Are you going to find my mommy and daddy?

Oliver turned back to Alex. "You said Teddy's dad was driving him to his mother's place in Victoria that night. That means only his father was in the car with him. I wish you'd told us Teddy's last name."

Alex flitted around Oliver's bedroom like a fairy before perching cross-legged at the foot of his bed.

I don't think I—you—wanted to remember back then. You have to find Teddy's parents. He's been pestering us to find them for over a decade. Then you can, like, concentrate on me. She threw the tails of her long red scarf over her shoulders and tossed her hair off her face.

Oliver sighed. "You have a point, squirt. Now, you two get off my bed and out of my head."

NINE

"WAKE UP, Olly. We've got to get on the road."

Sid nudged him in the back. He yawned and stretched. "Yup. I'm awake." He groaned.

Sid mumbled through her toothpaste. "Let's grab breakfast in Duncan."

"Yes, and gas." Oliver pulled on his jeans and a T-shirt. Sid insisted he keep a few extra "fresh" ones at her place, for her sake. He glanced out the window as he tied his laces. "It looks like it's going to be a nice day, finally."

She came out of the bathroom in her bra and panties. "Don't forget your computer."

"Got it." The green dress she took from the closet was one of Oliver's favorites. When she pulled it over her head, he smiled. She didn't wear it often enough to suit him.

"What?"

"Nothing. You look great, and you're always so bright and organized in the morning."

She bent over and gave him a kiss. "I have to be." She pointed at his toothbrush. "Hurry up. You can call your mom on the road."

* * *

OLIVER AND SIDNEY arrived in Victoria by mid-morning, in plenty of time to get into the *Times Colonist* archives. He opened his computer on the worktable. "Let's go to August 15, 2008. That's the day Mom and I drove up-island—the night of the accident."

Sidney searched through the stacks. "Okay. Here's August." She placed the folio binder on the worktable, removed the cover, and lifted the corner of each copy until she came to Friday the fifteenth.

Oliver flipped over Friday's edition. "It was late that night, so let's start with Saturday."

There was a big political rally on the Saturday, so the accident didn't make the front page, but there was a small article on the second page.

"A fatal single-vehicle accident occurred on the highway near Duncan Friday night, around midnight," Oliver read. "Heavy rain is thought to be a contributing factor. The driver was taken to Duncan Regional Hospital with life-threatening injuries. The four-year-old male passenger died at the scene. Names have been withheld… blah, blah, blah." Oliver pulled out his phone and took a photo of the article.

Standing behind him, Sid put her arms around his neck and kissed the top of his head. Through glassy eyes, he watched Teddy tugging at Alex's scarf. *Don't cry, Alex. Now we'll find my mommy, and you and Olly won't have to look after me anymore.*

Oliver had to grin. "That's right, Teddy. We should be able to find her now." He pulled Sid into his lap and kissed her. "We're getting warm."

Sid pulled his arms from around her and giggled. "Not that kind of warm." Wide-eyed, she opened the next issue and smiled. "Let's see if we can't find an obituary for you, Teddy."

But there was no obituary. Oliver closed the portfolio of August 2008 editions. "I don't get it. It should have appeared within a few days of the crash, since Teddy died at the scene."

Sid gave his arm a squeeze. "I know you're disappointed, Olly, but this is just a temporary setback." She looked at her phone. "Gosh, look at the time. No wonder I'm starving."

"Right." He folded his computer and stowed it in his bag. "We know Teddy's father was taken to a hospital in Duncan. If only Alex had told us his name... I think I was busy puking at the time." He placed the portfolio back on the shelf and grabbed his bag. "We can stop in Duncan on our way home, but right now, let's get over to Dad's. Lunch is probably ready."

* * *

THANKFULLY, his father hadn't gone through with the sale of Oliver's childhood home after the divorce. Oliver figured he had Meredith to thank for that. When they married, she had convinced him to keep the house and rent out hers furnished.

Sidney came to an abrupt stop in their driveway. Gripping the wheel, she looked straight ahead. "I want you two to behave yourselves for Olly's sake, okay? I know you can hear me." She grinned at Oliver. "Do you think they'll listen to me?"

Oliver leaned over and kissed her. "Oh, yeah. After all, they're in my head. It's up to me to keep them quiet." He scowled at Alex in the rearview mirror. She wrinkled up her nose at him while Teddy clutched his wet and dirty bear beside her.

* * *

CURTIS FRAMPTON MET his son at the door with a big hug and a slap on the back. "Good to see you, Oliver. Hi, Sidney. Come on in."

It still felt odd, after all these years, being invited into the house where he'd spent the first eight years of his life. "Thanks, Dad. I see you've made a few changes since I was here last."

Curtis took their coats and ushered them into the living room. "Well, Meredith has been doing a little redecorating. When she sold her house this spring, we kept the best pieces of furniture between us and decided to paint at the same time."

Sidney nodded. "She's pulled it all together nicely."

Meredith appeared from the kitchen, tea towel in hand. "I'm so glad you told us you were coming down today. Lunch is almost ready. What brings you to Victoria?"

Oliver leaned back on the sofa. "I'm doing research for an assignment. I had to access the archives at the *Times Colonist.*"

Curtis leaned forward in his chair. "What kind of research are you doing?"

"It's a criminology assignment in investigative journalism. I was looking for crimes that were never fully resolved in the papers. I need to apply my investigative skills." Oliver and Sid exchanged knowing grins. "Were there suspects, leads, arrests, convictions? That sort of thing. And about the victims. If they lived, what has become of them? How are they doing? Do they feel justice was served?"

Meredith reappeared. "Let's eat, everybody."

During lunch, his dad continued to probe for details. "That's fascinating, Oliver. I'm sure you will make a fine journalist. And Sidney, you're in the fine arts program, aren't you?"

"Yes, third year. I'm working on CG—I mean computer-generated—art right now."

Meredith refilled Sid's coffee. "There certainly is a vast market for CG art in the movies now. And I assume there are applications beyond my imagination."

"Absolutely. It will give me a career so that I can indulge in my first love: painting."

Curtis smiled at her and nodded to Oliver. "Smart woman." He pushed back his chair. "Well, let's move into the living room."

Oliver hadn't thought about Alex or Teddy once since entering his old home, but that changed in an instant when he turned to leave the table. There on a shelf behind him stood a picture of Meredith and Teddy.

And she was wearing Alex's red scarf.

* * *

SPEECHLESS, he grabbed the framed picture and tapped the glass repeatedly. Sidney squeezed his arm.

"Sit down, Olly." She guided him to the sofa.

Meredith sat next to him and took his free hand. "That's my late son, Teddy. Why is this of interest to you?"

Oliver gazed into Teddy's happy, smiling eyes. No longer sullen in wet pajamas, he wore jeans and a clean white shirt. "I've found you."

"Excuse me?" The look on Meredith's face was total confusion.

Sidney placed her hand on Oliver's back. "I think you'd better start at the beginning, Olly."

He handed the picture to Meredith and pointed at it. "I was there. I was there that night. August 15, 2008. It was the night my mother and I left this house." His father closed his eyes. "Sorry, Dad. We were driving to my Aunt Lila's place in Nanaimo. Leaving Dad like that terrified me. I didn't know it was going to be permanent. It was late at night, it was storming. Mom was crying, and visibility was almost zero. I was sure we were going to drive off the edge on one of those turns on the Malahat. Then I saw all the flashing lights. Mom told me to keep my head down. When a police officer in a yellow slicker waved us past…"

Meredith gasped.

"That's when I saw Teddy." Oliver could not hold back the tears. "He looked at me with such a peaceful look on his face."

His father raised Meredith from the sofa and wrapped his arms around her trembling body. The sounds emanating from the depths of her soul battered Oliver's heart.

Minutes passed, maybe more. The images of that night came flooding back—images he never wanted Meredith to imagine.

Sidney stroked his back, bringing him into the present, her soft voice dispelling the tension in his body.

"Meredith needs the closure only you can give her, Olly."

Oliver nodded. He rubbed his sweating palms on his thighs. He struggled to speak, but when he did, he explained as gently as he could how he had often visualized Teddy clearly since that night.

"I've always imagined that all Teddy ever wanted was for me to find his mother. I guess my eight-year-old mind came up with a solution to a circumstance over which I had no control." Sid smiled and nodded to him. Meredith deserved this believable version.

She smiled through her tears. "His name was Carlton Theodore Morgan, but we called him Teddy."

Oliver looked down at Teddy, playing at their feet. "You know, I can see him as clearly as if he were here in the room with us. And he is happy." He reached across and squeezed Meredith's hand.

Curtis passed a box of tissues, which helped lighten the mood in the room.

Meredith wiped her eyes and blew her nose. She smiled and patted Oliver's knee. "Even though my heart aches right now, your memory has given me a great deal of comfort, Oliver. This has obviously been an emotional journey for you. Thank you so much for sharing it with me." Meredith straightened and took a deep breath. "I think this calls for a toast." Within minutes, Curtis had produced a tray of glasses, a chilled bottle of wine, and a soda for himself. Meredith had helped his father conquer his demons as well.

After they had toasted the cathartic moment, Oliver leaned back and relaxed a little. "If you don't mind me asking, what happened to Teddy's father? I found an article about the accident that said he was severely injured."

Meredith stiffened. "He was in hospital for months, and then rehab, but he never went back to work. He's still living in Nanaimo now on a disability pension. That's why I had to rent out the house all these years. Teddy was gone, and he was in no position to pay alimony." She took a sip of her wine. "I visited him in the hospital once. I was so angry, I wanted to heap blame on his shoulders, but he was so badly injured I could only feel sorry for him.

"The day of the crash, he was supposed to be bringing Teddy home before supper. When he was late, I called. He said the babysitter hadn't brought him home yet, and he didn't know where they were. He was livid, and I feared what he would do when she got back."

While Meredith was speaking, Oliver was exchanging glances with Sid and Alex. He remembered well the day Alex had shared this haunting memory with him and Sid.

Meredith fidgeted with a tissue in her lap. "Apparently, she took Teddy to the movies because it was raining too hard to play in the park. I used to blame her when I couldn't blame Scott, but I had to let it go years ago." She smiled at Curtis.

Alex was sitting across the room, crying. He looked into Meredith's sad eyes. "Amazingly enough, I met that babysitter the same year. She blames—blamed—herself as well. She disappeared a year later."

Meredith held her breath. "Oh, how awful."

Oliver pointed at the picture in Meredith's lap. "Your scarf is beautiful."

"Thank you. It was unique. My husband bought it for me in Bali the year before Teddy was born. The year we separated, Teddy was three, and he loved that scarf so much I let him take it with him when he went up island to visit his dad." Her voice softened on a sigh. "I haven't seen it since he died, and I haven't the heart to ask Scott if he still has it."

Oliver exchanged silent words with Alex. *How did you come by it?*

Alex shrugged and led Teddy by the hand to his mother's side. *I honestly don't know, Olly.*

He almost laughed out loud. *Of course. Stupid question.*

"Meredith, I can imagine Teddy smiling up at you. And holding your scarf against his cheek." With a little wave and a smile, Teddy faded away.

TEN

OLIVER'S CHEST FELT HEAVY, and it wasn't the traffic in the Colwood crawl that made it so. He felt oddly sad now that Teddy was gone. Twelve years was a long time to have a four-year-old hanging around in his head. And, in recent years, Teddy's presence hadn't been as annoying as Alex's.

Just as they cleared the Malahat summit, Sidney interrupted his thoughts. "You're unusually quiet. That was pretty intense. How are you feeling about all this?"

Oliver rubbed his thighs. "Weird. He just faded away, and I haven't seen him since." He glanced in the back seat to be sure.

"But Alex is still here, though. Right?"

"Yes, and she looks upset. I think she's always felt guilty for his death. She never minded having him in tow all these years." He glanced in the rearview mirror. "I think she actually misses him."

"You said 'I think' there. As much as you've regressed since finding that article about her disappearance, you have maintained the right perspective about her. That's good, don't you think?"

"Think, think, think. I wish I could stop thinking." They drove on in silence.

* * *

IN BED THAT NIGHT, Oliver broke from Sid's embrace. He threw back the covers and sat on the edge of the bed, holding his head in his hands. "I can't tonight, Sid. I think I'd better go home."

Sidney dropped her feet over the side and put her arm around his shoulders. "What's wrong?"

Oliver shook his head.

"Is it Alex? Is she here because of all this... this emotional upheaval?"

Oliver flopped back on the bed, staring at the ceiling to avoid eye contact with Alex. He tried hard not to think of her when he was at Sid's. "I guess. But it's more than just Alex hovering around. It's this overwhelming sadness."

Sidney lay on her side, propping her head up with her elbow. She stroked his chest. "I think you are grieving for Teddy. After all, he's been with you for twelve years. It's understandable."

Oliver shook his clawed hands and hissed through his teeth. "Yes. But for most of those years, all I wanted to do was get rid of them. I had moments when I even fantasized about how to kill them, for god's sake."

"So, when you realized Alex may have been killed, you felt a little guilty, maybe? Add Teddy's departure to the mix, and what do you have?"

"Debilitating emotional turmoil?" He stroked her arm where it lay on his chest and sighed.

Sid touched her nose with her index finger and patted his pillow. "Come on, spoon with me. Your bedroom is more familiar territory for Alex. Alone with her there, you'll be awake all night." She climbed under the covers and held them open for Oliver. "She can sit on the end of the bed all night for all I care. She's grieving too."

* * *

THE MORNING SUN streamed in the kitchen window, giving the room a golden hue and turning Sid's hair to copper. It was warm when he kissed the top of her head. He poured himself a cup of coffee before sitting across from her. "Thanks for talking me into staying the night. I actually slept pretty well after the spoon ran away with the fork." Just as he knew she would, Sid blushed, making a feeble attempt to divert the conversation. He couldn't help smirking to himself.

"Do you think you should talk to Christine about this change in your... circle of friends? Does she even know about Alexis Young's disappearance?"

"She might have read about it back then, but she wouldn't have associated Alex's disappearance with me, because I kept up the pretense that Teddy was alone in my head."

Oliver slid a plate of eggs on toast in front of Sid and one for himself. "I haven't felt the need to see Christine since I graduated high school. Even then, it was just to set Mom's mind at ease. Don't worry. I think I can adjust to life without Teddy." He pointed at her untouched eggs with his fork. "Dig in."

"Right. Then I think you should focus on this assignment."

Oliver wiped his mouth and pushed his chair back. He pulled the photocopied articles, except the one about Alex's disappearance, out of his backpack and spread them on the table. He stabbed them with his finger. "I have these three to choose from."

Sid stacked the articles, turned them over with finesse, and motioned to his backpack. "Investigate Alex's disappearance for this assignment, Olly. You know you have to."

He turned away from her, his clenched fists pressed into the table, ignoring the sunbeams that had so recently brightened his morning. "You and Alex. She almost convinced me, too."

"You mean *you* almost convinced *yourself*." Sid tapped her temple.

"Okay. Yes. But I shouldn't do this, Sid. I can't keep our history out of the narrative. A professional journalist doesn't insert himself into the news."

"You don't want to find out if she's dead or alive? If she's homeless, on skid row, or buried in a shallow grave somewhere?"

"For chrissake, Sid. Of course I do, but how do I investigate without casting suspicion on myself? Don't you think people—like the police, for instance—will wonder why I withheld information for twelve years?"

Sid stood with her hands on her hips. "All right, give up. Live with this fifteen-year-old popping into your mind whenever you're stressed. Live with the realization you would rather talk to yourself through Alex than talk to me."

Olly's jaw dropped. After a few moments of tense silence, he nodded. "I do that, don't I?"

Sid inhaled and tossed her head.

Olly glared daggers at Alex, who sat on the counter swinging her feet. He rose and wrapped his arms around Sid. "I am so, so sorry. You know me so well. If I don't get Alex out of my head, she will always come between us, won't she?"

"I really think so, Oliver." Sid pulled his face down to hers and kissed him. "Let's go for a ride. Clear the cobwebs."

* * *

OLIVER AGREED. A hike up Sugarloaf Mountain would get those endorphins flowing and help him be more objective about Alex. He changed into his cycling clothes while Sid packed a lunch. He sighed. *If nothing else, this might clear the air between us.*

By the time they'd reached the summit, his gloom had lifted. He dropped to the ground beside her. "You were right. I feel much better."

She kissed him. "You're welcome."

The view of Departure Bay from the top was always breathtaking. A blanket of sequins glistened off the water. The ferry's warning horn sounded as it approached the terminal, its schedule uninterrupted on this fine day.

"Maybe you can clarify your thoughts in this light." She opened her arms to the sea.

Oliver chomped on his sandwich like a ravenous dog. The chewing gave him time to think. "If I'm going to do this, I'll definitely need your feedback to maintain objectivity." He glanced at Sid for her agreement.

She nodded with an enthusiastic grin. "No ifs about it."

"Okay, then. I think the first thing I have to do is establish if there were any signs, verbal or otherwise, that Alex *didn't* intend to move to Campbell River with her foster parents that weekend. We'll have to talk to them. She certainly didn't give any indication to us, did she?"

"That's true. So... the fresh air has done its job." She smiled at him sideways, popped the tab on a can of water, and handed it to Oliver. "What was their last name?"

"I have no idea."

"How is that possible? You used to bike all the way to Alex's place sometimes."

He shook his head. "It never occurred to me to ask her. I was eight."

"Yeah. I didn't ask her either." Sidney perched on a boulder. "And I suppose she can't tell you now." Oliver shook his head and gazed out over the bay.

Sid shrugged. "Where will you start?"

"Well..." He leaned on his knees. "I guess I'll check online for Alexis Young or any 'A. Youngs.' But I doubt it will be that easy." He burped. "Excuse me. Then I guess I'll go to social services. They should have a record."

Sidney tapped his back with the toe of her runner. "What was the name of the reporter who wrote that article?"

Oliver patted his shirt pockets before digging through his backpack. "It was... Here it is. Uh, Houston. Philip Houston. Good call. Let's hope he's still around."

Sidney rose and wiped the seat of her pants. "Well, Mr. Investigative Reporter, let's get down off this mountain so you can do some preliminary sleuthing online."

Oliver stashed their lunch bags in his backpack. "Right. Do I have a clean T-shirt at your place for class tomorrow? I'd like a do-over of last night."

Without skipping a beat, Sid said, "If you don't, you can wear that one in the shower. I'll help you soap it up."

ELEVEN

MONDAY AFTER CLASS, Oliver biked down to the *Nanaimo Observer* office, greeting the receptionist with a smile. "Hey, Nora. Do you know if a Philip Houston is still working here?"

"I don't recognize the name. How long ago are we looking?"

Oliver puckered up his face. "Twelve years?"

"That's way before my time. I think you need to talk to Sheila in HR."

"And she is...?"

"Second door on the right."

"Thanks, Nora." Oliver sprinted down the hall and knocked lightly on the Human Resources door.

"Come in."

Oliver introduced himself and asked Sheila about Philip Houston. He was feeling more and more like a bona fide reporter.

"Have a seat, and I'll see how far back my records go." Her fingernails clicked on her keyboard like an eager dog on a tile floor. The image was so clear in Oliver's mind he had to smile.

"Well, you're in luck," Sheila said. "He retired from the *Observer* five years ago. He was young, though. It looks like he retired for health reasons."

"That's great—well, not great, but do you have a forwarding address for him?"

Sheila shrugged and shook her head. "I do, Oliver, but I can't give it to you. Sorry."

"That's all right. But maybe you could tell me who I should speak to about an article he wrote back in 2009."

"Right. I think you should talk to Tom first. Then he may send you to the archivist."

Oliver rose and shook Sheila's hand with gusto. "Thank you very much, Sheila. I can find my way."

Oliver knew the editor, Tom Foreman. Tom was the one who'd singled Olly out at a lecture to submit one of his essays. He'd had a few of his historical 'interviews' published in the *Observer* since then.

Tom saw him coming down the hall and waved him in. "Oliver, good to see you. What are you writing these days?"

Oliver shook Tom's outstretched hand. "Good to see you, too. I'm working on an investigative assignment for a criminology paper."

"Interesting. What is the assignment?"

"To find an article about a crime that didn't appear to be resolved either in the media or the courts. I've found a few, but one stands out for me because it involves the disappearance of one of my childhood friends."

Tom sat behind his desk and indicated the chair opposite for Oliver. "Do you have the article with you?"

Oliver pulled it out of his backpack. "It's from twelve years ago, and I just came from Sheila's office. She tells me Philip Houston left your employ five years ago."

Tom was silent for a few moments as he read. "Yes, Philip succumbed to his illness shortly after taking early retirement. Very sad."

Oliver's heart sank. "I'm sorry to hear that, and not just because I was hoping to talk to him about this case. There was no follow-up for this article other than a short piece saying the police had suspended their search and reclassified Alex from a missing person to a runaway."

"Hmm. You say this Alexis Young was a childhood friend of yours?"

"Yes. She was fifteen, and I was almost nine, when she disappeared. I know that sounds odd, but we lived on the same street and walked to and from school together. She was fierce when it came to bullies."

Tom lapsed into his British accent. "Difficult to believe a strapping lad like yourself was bullied."

"I was pretty scrawny then. Being new to town, and with my family broken up... I had a fragile psyche at eight. I guess I was fair game, but Alex was a popular fifteen-year-old and didn't put up with any bullshit." Oliver leaned on Tom's desk. "I knew her pretty well, and I don't believe she was a runaway. The day after she disappeared, she was supposed to move to Campbell River with her foster parents. She didn't particularly want to relocate, but she wasn't so upset about it she would run away. Where would she go if what she really wanted was to stay in Nanaimo? It doesn't make sense."

Tom looked over his glasses. "This article doesn't include the foster parents' names. I wonder if Philip would have had them in his notes. Let me call Alan, the archivist in Records." He picked up the phone. "Did they interview you at the time?"

Oliver shook his head just as Alan came on the line. Tom asked him to look for Philip's notebooks and hung up.

"You're saying the police didn't even interview you, a close friend of Miss Young's?"

"Nope. As you can see, they interviewed her classmates, but they were high-school kids. I was in grade three. And I didn't question her disappearance because I thought she'd moved to Campbell River." Oliver glanced at Alex sitting on the corner of Tom's desk. He turned his head to ignore her.

"The amazing thing is, I saw her after school that day. It was the last day of school, so I know exactly what she was wearing. Neither this article nor the follow-up mentioned what she was wearing. Why not?"

"You're on to something there, Oliver. This will be perfect for your assignment. You have a way of getting the reader to feel they really know the subjects of your interviews." Tom leaned back in his chair and laced his fingers behind his head. "But I have to warn you. Since you were a friend of this girl, you may have trouble maintaining a professional perspective if you discover she came to a bad end. And you may not resolve the case at all." He nodded through knitted eyebrows. "Don't expect to tie this up with a pretty pink bow."

Oliver sat, silent. How had he let Sid talk him into this? Of course, this wouldn't have a happy-ever-after. *Shit.*

Just then, Alan appeared at the door with a dusty storage box labeled *Philip Houston*. He plunked it on Tom's desk.

Tom whipped off the lid, sending a cloud of dust into the air. They both stepped back, waving at the air in front of their faces. "Sorry. You take a bunch, and I'll take a bunch. The dates are on the covers. It's 2009, you said?"

Staring at a jumble of reporter's notebooks and file folders, Oliver tried to hide his nervous excitement. He nodded and grabbed a stack. Every notebook had a start and end date on the cover. As he examined the dates, he set them aside on Tom's desk. He flipped one open just to see what kind of note-taker Houston was. His heart sank. "This guy had his own little shorthand. I hope you can read it."

"Don't worry," Tom said. "He will always spell out names and places in full." He held a notebook aloft. "And here it is, or at least one from 2009."

Oliver couldn't stand it. He came around the desk to look over Tom's shoulder as he flipped the pages. Tom glanced back at the article for the date. "Bingo. Here it is. Alexis Young, age fifteen. Foster parents Glenda and Rob Render, names to be withheld pending investigation. And the rest is in the article."

Oliver glanced at the spelling and entered the names on his phone. "This is fantastic, Tom. I thought I might have to deal with social services to get these names." He pocketed his phone and slung his backpack over his shoulder. He shook Tom's hand and headed for the door.

"Hold up here one minute."

Oliver turned. "What?"

"A good reporter puts the research documents back the way he found them." He pointed at the box and all the notebooks strewn across his desk and raised his eyebrows.

Feeling more than a little sheepish, Oliver tossed everything back in the box and gently replaced the dusty lid. As he headed for the door a second time, he turned back. "Uh, where...?"

Tom smirked at him. "Ask Nora. She'll point you in the right direction."

Oliver felt his face flush as Tom's chuckle followed him down the hall.

* * *

ARRIVING HOME BY LATE AFTERNOON, Oliver fished his laundry out of his backpack and jammed it into the washer. He frowned at his jeans and stripped them off. They were getting a little stiff after a week. Stoked with the success of his first foray into investigative journalism with—hopefully—a live subject, he hummed to himself as he bounded upstairs to take a shower. To prevent Alex from invading his privacy, he controlled his thoughts.

He heard the front door open as he toweled off. He tied the towel at his waist and hustled down the hall to his room. "Mom, that you?"

"Yes. You're home. What happened? You run out of clean clothes?"

Oliver grinned. "Something like that. I'll be down in a minute."

He dressed and gathered up his grungy clothes from the bathroom floor. As he passed through the kitchen, he kissed her on the cheek. "You know me too well."

She smiled. "Are you staying for supper? Brad is coming over. Apparently, he has some big announcement."

"Really. That should be interesting."

"Now, Oliver, be nice."

Oliver rocked his head from side to side as he stuffed the washing machine and turned it on. He and Brad had never reconciled. Scratch that—Brad had always treated him like shit and annoyed Alex. It had been an immense relief to him, and Alex, when Brad moved out. Even then, Oliver had never fully relaxed until his mom took over Brad's room.

"Is there coffee, Mom?"

"Yes, help yourself."

Oliver sat, enjoying his coffee. They chatted while she made supper and his washing gyrated. He was itching to tell her about his assignment, but he didn't want to be interrupted by Brad, so he bit his tongue.

Aunt Lila arrived before Brad in a flurry. "Oh, Lauren. I'm sorry I'm so late. What can I do?"

"Nothing. It's all ready. Maybe just set the table. Oliver, put your feet down and give a hand."

The food was on the table when Brad burst in. "Am I late?"

His mother smiled. "Right on time, Son."

Everyone waited for his big announcement with differing degrees of curiosity. Brad was milking it for all it was worth, grinning at his mom throughout the meal. As she cleared the plates, she said, "All right, what's your big news?"

"I'm moving back home."

Oliver and his mother exchanged wide-eyed glances. Aunt Lila slid onto her chair in stunned silence. Then she spoke. "Why? What's happened?"

"They let me go. I didn't like that job, anyway. But now I'm behind with my rent, and I have to move out. It was a dump anyway."

Aunt Lila looked flushed. "I don't understand. Why would they let you go?"

Brad started picking his teeth with his fork. "Meh. Let's just say I had a little misunderstanding with the bitch who worked on my floor."

"Brad! Watch your language."

He sneered. "Well, it's true." He turned to Oliver. "You'll back me up, Olly. You remember Georgia? She was that so-called BFF of Alex's who moved in on Cole the minute that little skank friend of yours disappeared."

Oliver's chair clattered to the floor when he stood. "I've had just about enough of you and your foul mouth, Brad. You hated Alex because she wouldn't give you the time of day."

Brad puffed out his chest. "There's a lot you don't know about your precious little Alex. We hooked up before she left."

"You're lying." Oliver could hardly keep from belting him. He wished he could comfort Alex, who was cowering in the corner.

Brad saw his clenched fists and came nose to nose. "You think you can take me?"

His mother reached across the table and grabbed his arm. "Brad, sit down and shut up."

Oliver's mom pulled him back. "We will not have a brawl here in the kitchen."

Brad yanked his arm from his mother's grasp and strutted around the kitchen like a rebuffed rooster. "This is my home—my home! There isn't room enough in this house for both of us."

Aunt Lila crossed her arms, a forlorn look on her face. "Oliver, what can I do? You've never gotten along, and now... Well, this is an untenable situation."

Oliver's mom stood in front of him. "Lila! What are you saying? Are you kicking my son out? This has been our home since he was eight!"

"Well, what can I do, Lauren? This is my house, and Brad is my son."

"But I've paid my fair share so that you could *keep* this house after Arthur died."

Oliver took his mother by the arms and backed her away from

her sister. "Mom, Mom. It's okay, I'll move in with Sidney, and you can have my room. It'll be fine. I'd just as soon not live under the same roof with him again anyway." He wasn't about to let Brad control the situation. He wrapped his arms around his mother and felt the warmth of her silent tears on his chest.

* * *

THAT WEEKEND, Oliver cleared out his room to accommodate Brad. His mother and aunt were hardly speaking, which made the days leading up to the move extremely awkward. While they were loading Sid's beater, Brad drove up. He probably wished he hadn't after the dressing down he got from Sid. Oliver had to step between them to defuse the situation.

After they had stashed the last box in Sid's apartment, she flopped onto the sofa. "Your aunt is a piece of work. How she can let that sorry excuse for a man manipulate her like that is beyond me."

Oliver leaned against the kitchen counter. "Are you having second thoughts about me moving in?"

Sid leaped to her feet and into his arms. "Never. I just hate the way they treated you. And your poor mother having to stay there. It's going to be hard on her. I know she feels like she's abandoned you."

He held her close and stroked her back. "I know. But our moving in actually kept Aunt Lila from losing the house after Uncle Arthur died. Mom could have bought a condo with the divorce settlement, but she chose to help her sister out."

"Well, she doesn't owe her sister any loyalty now." Sid slapped her hands on Oliver's chest. "I'm going to be late for work. I've cleared out part of the closet and some drawers, but we may need to buy another dresser. See you later." She kissed him and hustled out the door.

He smiled to himself. Sid had made space for him in her closet. His wardrobe was meager compared to hers, but he definitely had more books. After he had stowed the contents of the boxes marked *clothes*, he came to one his mother had packed. When he popped the flaps, there was Brad's old bear. "Oh, Mom. You can't still believe this was Teddy." He tossed it into an empty box reserved for garbage.

* * *

IT TURNED out it was easier for Oliver and Sid to adjust to living together than it had been to coordinate their lives living apart. Since Sid worked evenings and on Saturday, Oliver was in charge of meals and shopping. He was also becoming quite efficient at ordering takeout. They converted the living room into an art studio and an office. There, late into the night, they worked on their respective assignments in harmony. They reserved Sundays for sleeping in and leisure... except this Sunday.

The sky was still dark when Oliver shook Sid awake. "Come on, Sid. We want to be there and back before class on Monday."

"Hmff. What time is it?"

"Five thirty. Come on. Here's your coffee. We'll grab breakfast on the way."

Sid dragged herself to the bathroom and brushed her teeth. "Do they know we're coming?"

"Not today specifically." Oliver had been grooming the Renders via email in anticipation of this visit, but he neglected to mention a date.

Sid splashed her face with cold water and dressed between sips of coffee. "Do you know if they'll even be there?"

"Pretty sure?" He handed her a commuter mug as she pulled on her coat.

"Olly, I'd better not be up at five thirty on a Sunday for nothing."

"Don't worry. I'll drive, and you can sleep all the way up." He pulled her lapels closed and kissed her.

"Now you're talking." Sid slipped into the passenger seat and pushed it back. Before Oliver was out of the parking lot, she was fast asleep again.

He smiled and adjusted the mirror. For three weeks, he'd been planning this trip to Campbell River. Remembering how he'd gotten Glenda's email address, he grinned to himself. Accidentally on purpose, he'd run into Georgia outside Brad's old workplace.

Since she had been a close friend of Alex's when they were kids, perhaps she knew how to get in touch with the Renders? Oliver's casual demeanor had taken Georgia aback. He wasn't about to let on he hadn't forgotten about Cole's relentless bullying and her part in it when they were young.

At first, she seemed suspicious, but Oliver leaned against the wall and crossed his ankles, trying to appear as disinterested as possible. Georgia soon shared her every thought. She didn't think Alex was dead. She was sure Alex had run away. When Oliver revealed he knew how Brad was fired, she started backpedaling. Anyway, she didn't have a clue how to get a hold of the Renders and doubted there would be anyone left in the old neighborhood who would even remember Alex.

That day, Oliver grinned to himself and waved to Georgia as he drove away. *Thank you, Georgia.* That last remark had given him an idea. Why *not* check with the Renders' old neighbors?

When he did, an elderly lady came to the door in her slippers and housecoat. Odd for that time of day, but whatever. You never know.

"Hello. I was a friend of Alexis Young when she lived next door. I lost touch when she moved to Campbell River. Do you have a contact phone number for her foster parents?"

"No, dear, we didn't keep in touch. You know that poor girl went missing at the same time?"

"Yes, I heard something about that. Do you know anyone else who may have kept in touch?"

Actually, she did. The man who ran the corner store at the time had since died, but his wife was still alive, and she and Mrs. Render were good friends.

Did she know where that lady was now?

"Yes, dear." She pointed to the house across the street. "She lives right over there."

Oliver thanked her and jogged across the street.

He had to suffer through a cup of tea with the widow before she gave him Glenda Render's email address.

The highway slipped away as he recalled that whole episode. When a Tim Hortons appeared ahead, he glanced at Sid, her head gently rocking as she slept. He shook her knee. "Breakfast?"

TWELVE

SID SQUEEZED Olly's arm as he knocked on the Renders' front door.

He bobbed his eyebrows at her. "Here goes. This beats interviewing long-dead historical figures."

The rotund woman who opened the door frowned. "Yes?"

Oliver gulped. She obviously wasn't expecting anyone. Maybe this wasn't the smartest course of action. "Mrs. Render?"

She nodded. "Yes. Who are you?"

"I'm Oliver Frampton, Alex's friend from Nanaimo. I've been emailing you."

A gravelly voice came from within. "Who is it, Glenda?"

She yelled over her shoulder. "It's that Frampton boy. You remember. Alex's friend." She turned back to Oliver. "What brings you up here?"

"Oh, we came to visit some friends camping on the spit and thought we'd drop by and say hello, since we were in the vicinity." He rocked from one foot to the other. *Is she going to leave us standing on the front step?* "Could we come in?"

Glenda Render looked over her shoulder. "I guess that would be all right." Although she held the door open wide, it left very little room for Oliver and Sid to squeeze by.

"Thank you, Mrs. Render. This is Sidney Wheeler. She and I were both friends of Alex."

Mrs. Render scooped newspapers and cats off the sofa. "We weren't expecting company so early in the morning. Excuse the mess."

Mr. Render took his feet off the ottoman and laid his newspaper aside. "Alex's friends, eh? How old were you when we left Nanaimo?"

Oliver pointed at Sid and himself. "We were both eight, a lot younger than Alex, but we often walked to and from school together. I lived just a few blocks away from you on Dufferin. Alex was very kind to us little kids."

"A bit too friendly to all the boys, if you ask me." He snapped his newspaper up in front of his face again, embarrassing his wife.

"Uh, would you like a cup of coffee?" she said.

Anything to stretch out this visit, Oliver thought. "Yes, please."

Mr. Render handed her his empty cup from behind his paper. "Here. I haven't had my second cup yet." His wife took it and disappeared into the kitchen. He never once interrupted the ten minutes of awkward silence that followed. But when his wife returned with a tray, he stood and left the room without a word.

She turned when the back door opened. "Rob, your coffee." The back door closed, leaving Mrs. Render standing in the middle of the room with the tray. She set it on the coffee table, took his cup, and sat in his chair. "Oh, well, I may as well drink his since he's gone out to his shop."

Sid tried to smooth over the abrupt departure of Mr. Render. "What type of work does your husband do?"

"Oh, this and that. He used to work at the mill, but since it closed, he's just been doing maintenance work at a couple of apartment blocks. It keeps him busy."

Oliver wanted to get the conversation back to Alex. "That mill job was why you moved here, wasn't it? I seem to remember Alex mentioning it."

"Yes. Please don't mind my husband. We haven't been able to foster any more children since Alexis's disappearance. They questioned us mercilessly about it, as if we were responsible."

"That must have been awful for you." Sid added cream and sugar to the brim of her mug and glanced at Oliver. She never took anything in her coffee, but this stuff looked like molasses.

"Yes, it was. I realize she was our responsibility, but no more than any other parent. Anyway, we were considered unfit to foster after that, and Dad hasn't gotten over it. You see, we couldn't have children of our own."

Oliver cleared his throat after testing the coffee. "That seems harsh. Alex was happy living with you. She never had an unkind word to say about her life with you."

"Thank you. That's very nice of you to say."

After a thoughtful moment, Oliver asked, "What ever happened with the search for Alex?"

Mrs. Render fidgeted. "The police decided she ran away, so they didn't really look very hard for her. I hope she did run away with that Brad who kept hanging around. I don't like to think of the alternative."

Sid looked at the floor, the corners of her mouth dropping like a marionette's. Oliver swallowed hard. "Uh, Brad is my cousin, Mrs. Render. And he's still living in the same house in Nanaimo."

Mrs. Render seemed to hold her breath for a moment before exhaling. "Well, that leaves one's mind nowhere else to go, does it?" She dabbed the corner of her eyes with a tissue.

"Indeed." Sid rubbed her hands on her thighs and offered an almost imperceptible nod toward the door.

"I'm sorry to have upset you, Mrs. Render. That wasn't my intention." Oliver set his coffee cup back on the tray. "I'd like to visit longer, but we do have to get on the road."

She nodded.

As they worked their way to the door, Oliver said, "I'd like to think Alex is alive and well somewhere, so I will continue searching."

Mrs. Render brightened. "You will?"

* * *

THEY WERE at the curb before Sid broke the silence. "That poor woman."

"I agree. But I can see why they weren't allowed to foster again. That guy has seriously deficient people skills." A sense of ambivalence welled up in him—not anger, but something else.

Sid glared at him over the roof of the car. "Oliver, if a child disappears from a biological family, their ability to parent their other children isn't questioned."

"You make a valid point. I really don't know the answer." He resolved to be nonjudgmental. After all, he aspired to be a professional journalist. He'd better think like one.

Sid broke the silence that followed them out of town. "Maybe Mrs. Render served the social worker that vile coffee."

Oliver turned into a Tim Hortons. "Let's see if we can't put that taste behind us." He turned off the key and leaned back. "You know, I didn't see Alex once when I was in their house."

"That's interesting. Like she didn't belong there."

"Hmm. Maybe." He looked at Sid's disapproving expression.

"What? I'm not judging them. It's just unfamiliar territory to *me*. I just can't visualize her there. Come on, let's eat." He pushed the car door open all the way to get his long legs out.

Oliver ordered the chili, and Sid ordered a chicken wrap. They ate in silence until Oliver spoke. "What did you make of Rob Render's comment about Alex being too friendly with boys?"

Sid sipped her coffee. "Mmm. That's better." She took a bite of her chicken wrap before answering. "You know, I thought at first he sounded like a typical father—no boy was good enough for his daughter. But when he took off without a word, I wondered. He didn't seem interested in discussing Alex's disappearance."

Oliver nodded. "I got the same vibe. And he really resented the fact that the police questioned him. Do you suppose he was a suspect?"

"Could be. They usually rule out family and friends first."

"They didn't question me, and I may have been the last person to see her alive… or whatever." He wished he hadn't said that. Alex looked abandoned, sitting at an empty booth.

Where are you, Alex?

* * *

THE NEXT SUNDAY, Sid stood at her easel, watching Oliver at his laptop. "You're staring at a blank document, and I'm staring at a blank canvas. Let's take a break and go for a ride to the park."

Oliver closed his laptop and spun out of his squeaking chair. "Good idea. I'm getting nowhere here."

A brisk wind made the fir trees moan as they neared the spot where Alex had jumped onto his handlebars that fateful night. He stopped.

"Tired already?"

"No. This is the spot."

"What spot?"

"The spot where I first imagined Alex." He looked into the trees. "Of course, I thought she was real when she popped out of those bushes onto my handlebars and scared the living shit out of me. She rode like that all the way to her place."

"Whoa! I'll bet that got your mojo up."

"I was in heaven. When I got home, I was changing into my pajamas when she just appeared, sitting on the bed. Until that moment, I thought the last half hour with her had been real."

"You know, I knew you had a crush on her back then, and I was jealous as hell."

Oliver wrapped his arm around her where she stood straddling her bike. "And it took another—what?" He kissed her. "Nine years for me to clue in?"

"I wonder what Christine made of all that turmoil in your little boy brain."

"Hell, I never shared that with her. Come on."

They stopped again at their bench by the duck pond. Sid took a long drink from her water bottle. "Tell me the last thing you remember about Alex that you know was real."

Oliver rested his arms across the back of the bench and frowned. "I remember being late exiting the school. Alex should have been halfway home by then, but then I saw her coming around the corner with Georgia. I raced out the back gate to meet her. She smiled and said, 'Where's your backpack?' I'd forgotten it at the bike rack. I started running back for it when she called out to me. She said, 'I'm not going home right now, Olly. Some of us are getting together at Connie's for the last time.'"

"So she had to be real because she was with Georgia."

"Right."

"And no one interviewed you about her disappearance."

"Right again."

"So go to the police and get them to reopen the case."

Oliver huffed. "Uh, no. What am I going to say? I know when and where Alex Young disappeared? That will land me in jail or the psych ward."

"That's ludicrous, Olly. You approach them as a journalism student on assignment. When you get their attention, tell them you were a friend of Alex's and you were never interviewed in their initial investigation."

Oliver rocked his head and stared into the middle distance. "Feasible."

"Of course it is. You just have to stay in character—be the investigative journalist you aspire to be."

"Keep talking."

"If you stay in character, you won't accidentally refer to Alex in her imprinted state."

Oliver rose and pulled Sid to her feet. "And once I get their attention, I can dig for info on all these other suspects."

"Now you're talking." They mounted their bikes and headed for home.

Alex rode his handlebars home. *She's not so bad, Olly.*

* * *

MONDAY EVENING, Oliver had just started the dishwasher when his phone rang.

"Hello."

Staff Sergeant Jameson from the Nanaimo RCMP detachment was returning his call. "You're a journalism student at VIU. Is that correct?"

"Yes. I'm researching the disappearance of Alexis Young twelve years ago for a criminology assignment." Oliver paced like an expectant father.

"Right. I've pulled the file. She was determined to be a runaway. The police interviewed her family and friends."

"Not all of them, Sergeant."

"Excuse me?"

"I was a friend of hers, and they did not interview me."

"How old were you at the time?"

"Eight."

"And you were a friend of this fifteen-year-old girl?"

"Yes."

"You're saying your interest in this case is personal, not just professional."

"Yes. I think I can bring a unique perspective to this assignment."

"You're right there. I'll give you that."

Oliver held his breath and waited.

"Mr. Frampton, I'd like you to come down to the detachment for an interview. If it reveals any new leads, we may reopen the case."

"Call me Oliver, please. And, yes, I can come in any day after four."

"Well, the sooner the better, so I'll see you tomorrow at four thirty."

Oliver thanked him as calmly as he could, leaped over the back of his chair, and booted up with the glancing jab of an orchestra director.

THIRTEEN

TUESDAY AT FOUR FIFTEEN, Oliver leaned his bike against the wall of the RCMP entrance. A no-nonsense officer dominated the spartan foyer even from behind glass.

Oliver gulped. *This is it. You're a professional journalist, Oliver Frampton.* "Sergeant Jameson is expecting me. Oliver Frampton?" He scarcely had time to peruse the bulletin board before the sergeant opened a side door and ushered him into a stark interrogation room rather than an office.

"We're going to conduct this as an official interview, Oliver," Jameson began. "You are a material witness first and a journalism student second, so this will be recorded. You understand?"

"Yes, of course." Oliver scrutinized the imposing figure across from him. Jameson looked to be a fit forty-something, his hair graying at the temples.

He opened a thin file—a sad indication of the depth of the investigation into Alex's disappearance. He examined her photo for a moment before handing it to Oliver.

"Is this how you remember her?"

Oliver blinked and cleared his throat. "That is her school picture, but I remember Alex the way she was dressed the day she disappeared."

"Why do you remember how she was dressed that day in particular?"

He had to be careful. "Because I knew I might never see her again—she was moving to Campbell River the next morning. I was an eight-year-old with a crush. I took a mental picture so that I'd never forget her." Oliver shrugged.

Jameson looked at her photo upside down. "A crush, eh?" Oliver shrugged again, but he couldn't stop the heat rising in his cheeks.

To his relief, Jameson kept his eyes on the photo. "Describe this mental picture you took."

"She had on a pair of extreme jeans, with blowouts at the knees; a plain white T-shirt; runners; and a long red scarf." Oliver caught himself before he said any more about that.

"That's very specific. As clear as an actual photo."

"My thoughts exactly when I realized..."

"When, exactly, did you make this realization?"

Oliver handed Jameson the photocopy. "When I came across this. For my assignment, I was going through back issues of local newspapers, looking for crimes that didn't appear to have any follow-up arrests or trials. That's when I found this article about Alexis Young. You can have that for the file. You'll notice it makes no reference to what she was wearing. That seems peculiar to me."

Jameson leafed through the file and raised his eyebrows. "Thank you." He clipped the article to the inside cover. "Occasionally, some detail is withheld, but in this instance..."

Oliver pointed at the file. "What's so bizarre is that Alex and I often walked home through the park together. Her friends all knew that, but they obviously didn't bother to tell whoever interviewed them. I mean, Georgia Boyland was with her when I last saw her."

Jameson's face didn't betray what had to be his irritation. Flip, flip through the file. Stop. Glance over a sheet. Close the file. Look up. Whatever he was looking for wasn't there. "Tell me about that last time you saw Alexis Young."

After Oliver had recounted the same story to Sidney in the park, she had insisted he document it, which he'd done that very night. That process had jarred even more detail from his memory. Thanks to Sid, his recollection was now crystal clear. When he had finished, Jameson leaned back in his chair and said nothing for several minutes. He glanced again at the sheet where his thumb was.

"This Georgia Boyland, friend of Alexis. What can you tell me about her?"

Oliver thought for a moment. "Well... back then, I would say they were best friends. But there was this senior, Cole Thomas, who was hot for Alex. She hung out with him a bit. They didn't go on dates per se. I mean, she was fifteen, and she said her foster parents wouldn't allow her to date. I'd see Alex and Cole go for walks to the duck pond. On one occasion there, Cole was giving me a hard time, and Alex stood up for me. They argued and basically broke up, but she was still heartbroken when he said he was taking Georgia to grad."

"What was this Cole Thomas giving you a hard time about?"

"Ah, just kid stuff, but Alex wouldn't tolerate bullying of any kind, so she stuck up for me."

"How was her relationship with Georgia Boyland after that?"

Oliver rubbed his thighs. "Here's the thing. The last day of school was a Friday, and the grad ceremony and dance were on the Saturday. By then, Alex had learned she was leaving the next day and would miss grad anyway. I think Cole only asked Georgia to grad to spite Alex because of their fight, and I think Georgia knew it. But she hung out with Alex all that last week of school. She was a fickle friend, to say the least. I can only speculate on her motives. Rubbing salt in Alex's wound, maybe?"

"You're right. That is speculation." Jameson opened the file at his thumb again. "Here's a name you may find familiar: Bradley Forrester."

Oliver jumped to his feet, and the pulse in his neck beat against his collar. "Brad is my cousin. We lived in the same house. You mean the police interviewed him, and he didn't mention me?" Oliver turned his head sideways, trying to see the file, but Jameson closed it before he could make out a word.

"It would appear so. He was interviewed along with other witnesses to an incident at Connie's Café in which Alexis Young was involved, so it was cross-referenced to this file." He flicked the corner of the report. "And there's no mention of you here."

"Brad was involved in an altercation with Alex?"

"No. He was a witness, along with Georgia Boyland."

"With Georgia? That had to be a coincidence, because he... he wasn't interested in Georgia." Oliver had to take a moment to regroup. Why was he there? *Of course. It was Brad's graduation too.*

Jameson interrupted his thoughts. "Is there anything else you can recall about Georgia?"

"I tracked her down just last week, and we had a lengthy conversation."

"Why last week?"

"I was looking for the name of Alex's foster parents. As you can see, their names do not appear in that article. Georgia got me thinking about the old neighborhood, and eventually I found someone who remembered them."

"You found *them*, or just their names?"

"Both. My girlfriend and I drove to Campbell River last weekend and visited them."

Jameson gave a lengthy sigh before asking for their names. Verifying them with the file, he rubbed his face with his hands and looked at the clock.

"Oliver, I think we need to have another meeting about this case. I have to go out of town for a week, and the case can't get any colder in that time, so I'd like you to schedule another session for the week after, with the constable at the front desk."

Oliver squinted at Jameson. "Sure. I just have one question."

"Ask away."

"What was the 'other matter' that came up when my cousin was interviewed?"

Jameson closed the file with finality. "Do you know a man that Alexis Young would have known at the time who used crutches?"

For the first time in the interview, Oliver lied. "Not that I can recall offhand." It could only be Scott Morgan, but Oliver wasn't prepared to implicate Teddy's father in Alex's disappearance—at least not yet. *How could Morgan's name not be in that file?* Oliver wanted to press Jameson for more details about the altercation, but the sergeant opened the door and waved him out. It would have to wait.

* * *

THAT NIGHT, Oliver waited up for Sid. It was eleven thirty when she dropped her backpack at the door. "I'm exhausted. The store was busy the entire evening."

Oliver rose from the sofa and propped her up. "I had that interview with Jameson today."

"Well, join me in the shower, and keep talking, because I'll be dead to the world when my head hits that pillow."

"I can do that." Oliver walked Sid into the shower like a marionette. But when he recounted the lie—the moment he'd learned that Scott Morgan, on crutches, had seen Alex that last day—Sid came alive. As they fumbled with towels and clothes, Oliver followed her to the bed. Sid bounced into a cross-legged position, wide awake.

"Tell me, tell me. What did he say about their encounter?"

"Not much. He called it 'an incident.' It was part of an interview with Georgia and Brad at Connie's after school that day."

"Georgia and Brad?"

"There must have been some sort of confrontation between Alex and Scott Morgan. Someone obviously called the police. Alex and Morgan—if that's who it was—had to have left before the police arrived, so they interviewed Georgia and Brad about it. I can't help wondering why they never followed up with Alex. If they had, who knows? She might be alive—I mean... Well, you know what I mean."

Sid pulled Oliver's face to hers. "I know that ever since you left Teddy with Meredith, you've wondered just how much Morgan blamed Alex for Teddy's death."

"Yes. I thought when this day came, I'd feel sympathy for him, but..." Oliver held up three fingers. "He had means: even on crutches, he was intimidating enough for someone to call the police. He had motive: even Alex blamed herself for Teddy's death. And he had opportunity. It had to be him. He was there at Connie's that last day—the last time I actually saw Alex."

* * *

EAGER TO INTERVIEW Scott Morgan before his scheduled meeting with Jameson the following week, Oliver decided it would feel less confrontational to visit him as a couple with Sid rather than showing up alone as a journalist.

Meredith had given Oliver an address. Apparently, when Morgan was in hospital all those months after the accident, it had been necessary for her to look after his affairs since they were still legally married at the time.

The day dawned foggy, lending an eerie chill to his plan. Sid drove with extreme caution to a seedy area of town.

"Oh. My. God. Look at that place." Sid pulled up in front of a dilapidated house. She turned to Oliver. "What do you think?"

"I think Scott Morgan has been on hard times for almost thirteen years. Let's start with a knock on the door."

A raspy voice hollered back after Oliver's third rap. "I'm coming, goddammit." The door squeaked open, and a man, looking much older than his years, wheeled around it. "What do you want?"

"Mr. Morgan, I—"

"How do you know my name?"

"Uh, I saw it in the paper recently. Well, not a recent paper. I was doing some research in old newspapers and found the report of your accident." Oliver glanced down at the wheelchair. Morgan's name hadn't been in the article, but it was just a small lie.

"So what's it to you?"

"Well, Mr. Morgan… uh… Could we come in for a minute to explain?"

"No, I'll come out." He struggled to get his chair over the threshold, but it was clear he had done it many times before. Morgan pulled a throw around his shoulders, perhaps having second thoughts after the morning chill set in. Sid zipped up her jacket to her chin. Leaves littered the creaking porch floor. There were no other chairs, and the railing looked rickety, so Oliver and Sid stood. It felt awkward looking down on him, but he seemed used to it.

"Mr. Morgan, the reason I wanted to see you was to tell you that, well, for all these years, I didn't realize that I saw your accident."

"How?"

"I was eight, sitting in the back seat of my mother's car as we drove from Victoria to Nanaimo, when I saw the flashing lights up ahead." Oliver looked at Sid for encouragement. She nodded.

"It was storming like…"

Morgan became agitated. "Don't you think I know that?" His unshaven face quivered and his hands shook. "My little boy died that night. He died!"

"But, Mr. Morgan, I want you to know that he died peacefully. He did not suffer."

"How would you know? You were eight!" Morgan spit the words at Oliver.

The pain that creased his face cut Oliver to the core. He bent over, half kneeling to be at eye level with Morgan. "I know, Mr. Morgan. I know. Because, if an eight-year-old on that stormy night had seen a little boy in distress, he'd have been traumatized, wouldn't he?" Oliver didn't wait for an answer. "But I wasn't. I wasn't. I remember Teddy closing his eyes as peacefully as if he were going to sleep in his own bed, with his teddy bear tucked under his arm." Oliver struggled to hold back his own tears, while Morgan made no effort to stem the flow of his. Even Sid turned away and dabbed her eyes.

Without warning, a growl emitted from the depths of Morgan's congested lungs that made them step back. "That bitch. She killed my boy. That bitch. I wish I had killed her then!" He turned his chair with a jerk and bumped over the threshold, slamming the door in Oliver's face.

Oliver's breath caught in his throat. His mind raced. When Sid pulled his limp arms around her, he watched over her shoulder as Alex fled into the fog, sobbing.

Sid pressed her keys into Oliver's hand as they walked stiff-legged back to her car. "You drive. I just want to go home."

This was not how he had envisioned the interview going. He climbed into the driver's seat and turned the key. "What did he mean, 'then'? Did he just confess? I should have asked him about that confrontation right then. Damn."

But the sight of Sid hugging her knees on the seat beside him told him to zip it.

Her lips trembled. "Let's just get home. I feel sick."

* * *

ENTERING their apartment was like stepping back through a portal from another century. He dropped Sid's keys on the counter. "I could use a beer. Do you want one?"

"Give me wine. Lots of wine."

"You got it." In minutes, he had their drinks poured. Sid snuggled up against his chest, each of them processing what they had just witnessed. They sipped their drinks in silence except for the ferry foghorn and the whirring of the refrigerator. Oliver contemplated the shitstorm he was in.

He broke the silence. "I've got to ask him. I'm going back."

"Oliver, you can't go back there. You should go straight to Jameson." She circled around Oliver and stood between him and the door.

"He won't be back until next week. My meeting with him is scheduled for Monday. I have to go back to Morgan's now. I want to see his face when I ask about the altercation at Connie's the day

Alex disappeared. Alex and Morgan both left before the police got there, so no one knows what happened after that." Oliver picked up her keys. "Are you coming with me or not?"

She stepped aside and crossed her arms. "No. This is a big mistake, Olly. You don't know what he's capable of."

"I'm not going to intimidate him. What's he going to do? He's in a wheelchair." He started for the door but looked back just in case she reneged. His resolve balked when she shook her head.

He argued with himself right up to the moment he knocked on Morgan's door. *This will be fine. I'll be cool, professional even.* But when Morgan opened the door, Oliver pushed past him.

"Mr. Morgan, I want to know. Who's the bitch who killed your son?"

Morgan became flustered, his words ragged. "It was… it was the babysitter. Alexis. Alexis Young. Sh-she, she had him that day, all day. She was supposed to have him home by five, but, but she took him to the movies instead."

His anger surfaced. "She never called me once to say where they were. No call. Nothin'. I was so spittin' mad when she waltzed in here close to nine. I could have killed her right then. I still had to take Teddy to his mother in Victoria in that storm. She'd already called. I was afraid I might not get Teddy again."

He rubbed the tears from his cheeks with the back of his gnarled fist. "I *should* have killed her right then." He took a framed photo from the table beside his chair. "Teddy kept this at his bedside when he stayed with me. That's his mother." He tapped the photo with a bony finger. "I bought that scarf for her in Bali. Teddy loved it, so she let him have it for comfort when he came here."

A simmering rage built in his voice. He slammed the photo face-down, breaking the glass. "When I saw that little bitch with that scarf around her neck that day, I, I grabbed it." Morgan snatched at the air. "She screamed, and a couple of kids ran at me. She wouldn't give it to me. A woman came out of the café and said she'd called the cops, so I left." He spit out the words. "That little bitch still has my Teddy's scarf."

Oliver couldn't breathe. "Did you follow her, Morgan?"

He looked up, confusion creasing his brow. "What?"

"Did you follow Alexis into the park that day?" Oliver could not help his menacing tone.

"What the fuck? You think I killed her? Huh? Huh?" He grabbed a cane and swung wildly, striking Oliver on the side of the head before he could even raise his arms. "Get the fuck out of my house. I'm calling the cops." Oliver stumbled out the door in a daze.

FOURTEEN

OLIVER AWOKE to the sound of knocking. He glanced at the clock: eleven thirty at night. He stumbled out of bed in his shorts and pulled on his jeans.

"Who is it?"

"Police. Open the door, Mr. Frampton."

Oliver opened the door, rubbing his eyes. "What's up? Is there a fire?"

"No. We'd like you to come down to the detachment, please. Get dressed."

Sid rushed out of the bedroom. "What's this about, Officer?"

"There's been a complaint made against you, Mr. Frampton."

It had to be Morgan. His mind buzzed with the what-ifs. Would Morgan have called the police if he were guilty? He frowned at Sid, who stood with her arms crossed, glaring back at him.

"This shouldn't take too long to sort out, Sid. I'll call you if I need anything." He finished dressing and nodded to the officer. Escorting Oliver out, the officer looked at the bandage on his head, and the spreading purple around it, but said nothing.

Oliver felt like a criminal riding in the cruiser's back seat. This was going to be a long night, and Jameson would not be pleased with these developments. Perhaps his second visit to Morgan hadn't been the wisest course of action.

In the interview room, Corporal Franks sat opposite. "What were you doing at Mr. Scott Morgan's house earlier this evening?"

"It's a long story, Corporal. That was my second visit to his house today. My girlfriend and I went to see him this morning about the death of his son. I think the Alexis Young file on Sergeant Jameson's desk will explain a lot."

"He's out of town until Monday."

"I know. I have another appointment to meet with him." Oliver's knee bobbed up and down as he waited.

Corporal Franks returned with the file twenty minutes later. "I do not see any mention of Scott Morgan in this file." He looked at the cover again. "This case is twelve years old. I'm not phoning Sergeant Jameson at this time of night. What is his interest in this case?"

Oliver explained how the journalism assignment he was researching led to his call to Jameson.

"After my interview with Sergeant Jameson, I got to thinking about the man on crutches that had been harassing Alex the day she disappeared. I remembered her telling me about a child she had babysat who died in a car accident after she'd brought him home late, and how the father had been badly injured. She told me he blamed her, which only added to her feelings of guilt."

"This man was Morgan? How did you deduce that?"

"I'm getting to it. My folks have been divorced since 2008, and I have regularly visited my father, who has since remarried, in Victoria. At his house, I recently saw a photo of his new wife and her son, who died in a car accident in 2008. That led me to link her son to Alex—Alexis. In the photo, she wore the same scarf that Alex wore on the day she disappeared. And that led me to her ex-husband, Scott Morgan."

"That doesn't explain why you went to visit him."

Oliver leaned on his elbows. "I was there, at the accident scene, when I was eight. I saw his son die on the road that night. But, because the boy looked like he was just falling asleep with his teddy bear tucked under his arm, I was not traumatized." The lie felt more and more like the truth every time it rolled off his tongue. "I thought that would be a comforting image to give Morgan. I thought he'd like to know that." Oliver sat back, pleased with the way he'd connected the dots.

"And your second visit?" Corporal Franks pointed to the bandage and bruising on Oliver's forehead. "What provoked that?"

Oliver touched the bandage and winced. "Morgan said something unexpected during that first visit. He was spewing his hatred for Alex when he blurted out how he wished he'd killed her *then*. Sid and I left in shock. We argued about whether or not to go straight to the police. She wanted to, but before we did, I wanted to ask him outright what he meant."

"You should have listened to your girlfriend. Harassing anyone, especially a disabled person, is a serious offense. And then there's the interference in a police investigation."

"There is no active police investigation. You wouldn't even have known about all this if I hadn't come forward with my investigative journalism assignment."

Deep in thought, the corporal stared at him for several moments before speaking. "Tell me about that injury."

"It happened when I asked him about the incident outside Connie's Café." Oliver pointed at the file. "It's all in there. He had confronted Alex about that scarf I was telling you about. She wouldn't give it to him, and he got aggressive. The police were called, but Alexis and Morgan were both gone by the time they got there. They interviewed two people who saw the incident." He pointed at the file again. "It's in there.

"When I asked him if he'd followed Alex into the park after that incident, he got violent and struck me with a cane. He threatened to call the police, but I didn't think he'd actually do it if he was guilty. Perhaps he thought you wouldn't see past his disability after all these years."

Corporal Franks glanced from Oliver to the Alexis Young file in his hand. "Do you plan to lay an assault charge against Scott Morgan?"

Oliver was taken aback. "Assault charge? No. I don't intend to heap any more grief on those narrow shoulders. If this case is reopened, and it turns out he was involved in Alex's disappearance, he'll have bigger problems."

Corporal Franks closed the file. "You're free to go for now, Mr. Frampton. Sergeant Jameson will see this interview before your meeting. Do I need to tell you to stay away from Scott Morgan?"

"No, sir, you don't."

* * *

AT THEIR SECOND MEETING, Jameson was furious. Oliver was sure everyone in the detachment could hear him from his office. And this time it wasn't a recorded interview.

"I can understand why you and Sid visited Morgan that day—the first time. But whatever made you think it was a good idea to go back and interrogate him?"

"I thought—"

"No. You didn't think." He slapped Alex's file on his desk. "When you volunteered more information on this case, it became an active investigation again, and your second visit to Morgan interfered with that investigation. Hell, even as an investigative reporter, you crossed the line." Jameson huffed.

"I'm sorry. I just couldn't believe my ears. What now?"

Jameson picked up the file and held the door open. "Now, we are going to go into an interview room, and we are going to record every bloody detail of those two visits to Morgan. And then you're going to tie this all together with a bright red scarf." Jameson jerked his head at Oliver. "Let's go."

* * *

THE AIR in the apartment all that week smoldered with tension. Jameson had called Sid in to confirm Oliver's version of events at the Morgan visit. When the paint hit the canvas with a slap, Oliver kept his nose close to the keyboard. His notes were a jumble of unconnected ramblings—few facts and even less corroborating evidence.

He leaned back, staring at the screen. His objective was not clearly stated. That was his first problem, because his professional objective so clearly conflicted with his personal objective: to rid his life of Alex, whose imprint interfered with his adult life in every way. Adjusting to Teddy's departure had been difficult, and now Alex... His ambivalence about her future with him kept him off-balance. How would he really feel if he could never visualize her again?

The phone rang. It was Jameson. The police were going to inter-view Brad, Georgia, Connie, and Scott Morgan this time. Along with any other witnesses to the altercation at the coffee shop that day.

Oliver hung up. "They are going to actively investigate Alex's disappearance." He cracked open a beer, sat on the sofa, and grinned, albeit a bit sheepishly.

Sid put down her brush and got herself a glass of wine before joining him. She clinked her glass against his beer. "This doesn't mean I'm not still mad at you." She took a sip. "What if he had connected with your temple?" She poked his bruise, which hurt more than he cared to let on. "Or your eye?"

"I know. You're right. I should have listened to you and let Jameson follow up. We only had a quasi-confession that we could have misinterpreted. Jameson probably could have gotten a full confession out of him. As it is, everything from Morgan is hearsay. That's my bad."

"You're missing the point, Olly. You could be blind or dead." She cuddled up under his arm. "And if you died, I'd never speak to you again... like Alex."

FIFTEEN

WHEN BRAD PUSHED past Oliver into the center of his living room, Oliver let it slide. Brad might have thought he could intimidate him, but he wasn't dealing with a little kid now. Jameson had interviewed Brad that morning, and 'cuz' was pissed. Oliver opened two beers, set one on the coffee table, and leaned back on the sofa.

"Have a seat. That's your beer."

Brad grabbed the beer but continued to fume. "What the hell are you doing, getting the police to open that old case? That was twelve fucking years ago!"

Oliver put his feet up on the coffee table. "It was for a criminology assignment, Brad." He wouldn't elaborate. Let the guy try to justify his indignation.

"You told them Scott Morgan killed Alex? That crippled guy?"

"I didn't say that. I now know Morgan drove to Connie's that day. He intimidated her. He got into a heated argument with her over a scarf. He tried to rip it off her neck. You were there. You saw it."

"Well, I didn't know who he was then, but I know he didn't follow Alex into the park. She walked away by herself, and he drove off in his car. After the cops left, I went looking for the guy's car. It took a while, but I found it parked at a dump of a house."

"But you never volunteered that information to the police?"

"He only grabbed her arm. It was nothing." Brad took a swig.

Oliver closed his eyes to visualize the overlapping timelines. Could Morgan have followed Alex into the park on foot—and crutches—without being seen, killed Alex, disposed of her body, and returned to his car in time for Brad to see it in front of his house? Not remotely possible.

Brad guzzled his beer and licked his lips. "Funny thing, though: I think Cole blew her off that day, too."

"Cole was there? The police didn't interview him."

"He was in the bathroom when Morgan grabbed her. How do you know they didn't interview him?"

"I brought the police additional evidence. Evidence that you neglected to tell them."

"What evidence? A little pissant like you." The insult didn't prevent Brad from making himself comfortable and drinking his beer.

"Give it a rest, Brad. You're a grown man." Oliver clicked his tongue. "Alex was my friend. That day, I met her and Georgia at the back gate, headed for Connie's."

"What kind of evidence is that?"

"I could tell them what she was wearing, and that she wasn't about to run away with someone. She didn't like the idea of moving to Campbell River, but she was going to."

"You had a crush on her, didn't you? You little shit. That's why you remember what she was wearing. I'll bet you undressed her every day with your eyes."

"That would be you, Brad. By the way, I didn't tell the police what you said at the house that day."

"What?"

"You remember. You told me you hooked up with Alex before she left. Maybe you didn't follow Morgan. Maybe *you* followed Alex into the park that day."

Brad jumped up and jutted his chin in Oliver's face. "I didn't follow her. And I wouldn't sleep with that bitch if she begged me."

Oliver smirked back at him, his rippled jaw the only sign of his inner rage. "Of course. You *couldn't*. Alex didn't have the time of day for you. Don't slam the door on your way out."

Storming past Sid in the doorway robbed Brad of that opportunity.

With a double take, Sid closed the door behind him. "What was that all about?"

Oliver rubbed his shaking hands over his face and shook his head. Without a word, Sid was there, stroking his back. It took him a few minutes to calm down. Hiding his anger had taken a lot out of him.

"I can't believe I held it together." He exhaled between gritted teeth. "Brad was pissed because I went to the police about Alex's disappearance and they called him in for an interview. He just told me that after the police left, he went looking for the guy's car. He didn't know who it was at the time." Oliver shook his head. "But he never gave that information to the police. It's rather convenient now, don't you think? If he did follow Morgan that day, he alibis him, but in doing so... he also alibis himself."

* * *

TWO DAYS LATER, Oliver and Sid were still debating whether to call Jameson.

Sid took the deli salad container out of the fridge and set it in the middle of the table. "Olly, I can't see what good it will do for you to talk to Jameson about your suspicions. Don't you think he would have realized the same thing when he interviewed Brad?"

"I guess it depends on whether Brad told them the same thing." Olly pulled the skewers out of the oven.

"I guess. But what about the irreparable damage it would do to your family dynamic? I mean, your mother still has to live under the same roof as Brad."

"I think all the damage that can be done has been done. Besides, Aunt Lila depends on what Mom contributes. She wouldn't want Mom moving out."

They sat down to eat. "All I'm saying is, it could get pretty frosty over there."

* * *

MONDAY MORNING, after Sid left for class, Oliver called Sergeant Jameson. He'd be late for class, and Sid wasn't going to be happy with him, but he had to know.

"Is this important, Oliver?"

"Not really. Cousin Brad dropped by after his interview with you. He was livid because I had instigated the reopening of Alex's case." Oliver paced around the table.

"You're right. This isn't important. Quickly, get to the point."

Oliver couldn't keep the agitation out of his voice. "Did Brad tell you he followed Morgan after the police spoke to him at Connie's that day? He followed the guy home but never told the police where he lived. From the plates, the police could have discovered his name and linked it to the car accident."

"Calm down, Oliver."

"I can't calm down." He couldn't keep his voice from rising. "Maybe Alex could have been found that day." He pounded the table with his fist. "And another thing: this supposedly alibis Morgan. Brad's not that bright, but he could have made this whole thing up to alibi himself."

"Are you finished?"

Oliver exhaled like a fizzling balloon. "Yes."

"Listen. I understand. But you must stop interfering with this investigation."

Oliver tried to stifle his indignation. "Brad came to *me*."

"This time. But you know what I mean. We will do the investigating, not you. And I mean that, Oliver. Leave Brad to me, and stay away from anyone remotely connected to this case. You are not yet an accredited member of the press, nor a licensed private investigator. Do I make myself clear?"

* * *

THAT EVENING, Oliver was licking his wounds and staring at his computer screen when his phone rang. This time, it was his dad.

"Son, we have a problem."

Oliver stood as if poised for some bombshell. "Are you sick?"

"No, nothing like that. It's this business with Scott Morgan."

"Morgan? What's that got to do with you?"

"You know he's Meredith's ex-husband?"

"Yes."

"He's accusing her of setting him up for Alexis Young's murder."

"But how?"

"By sending you to harass him and bringing the police down on him."

"That's ludicrous."

"Nonetheless, Meredith is very upset."

"I can imagine."

"So, Oliver… I want you to stay away from Scott."

"You don't have to worry about that, Dad. I just got off the phone with Sergeant Jameson. He's the one reinvestigating Alex's disappearance. And he's just lambasted me with the same warning."

"Oh, I'm sorry."

"But that doesn't mean the police won't talk to him again. I can't do anything about that."

"Of course not."

This development hadn't occurred to Oliver. "I'm sorry about this, Dad. Maybe call Jameson and tell him about Scott's accusation. If Jameson interviews him a second time, he may caution him against any further threats to Meredith."

"Yes. Right. I'll do that if he calls again." His sigh of relief was audible. "So, after all that, how is the assignment coming along?"

Oliver looked at the document in front of him, which contained only the words "What Ever Happened to Alexis Young?" at the top.

"Well, I think I've got the title nailed."

* * *

WHEN SID ARRIVED home from work that evening, Oliver looked at the time and jumped up from his computer. A new second monitor sat next to it. "I'm sorry, Sid. I was working on this damned assignment. We probably have enough leftovers to make a decent supper."

Sid dropped her backpack by the door and flopped on the sofa. "Anything's fine, Olly. Just make it quick. I'm going straight to bed."

In minutes, Oliver whipped out the leftover deli salad, added some chopped leftover ham, and topped it off with sliced hard-boiled eggs. He glanced over at Sid; she was asleep. He slipped her arms out of her coat, her feet out of her shoes, and carried her to bed. *Poor kid.* These evening shifts were wiping her out.

She roused long enough to say, "Wake me in an hour, okay?"

Oliver kissed her and turned out the light. As he covered the salad, he felt a little embarrassed about their arrangement. But Sid had been adamant that she was getting the better part of the deal: he would take on all the domestic chores while she worked. His appreciation of his mother rose with each load of dishes and laundry, and he tried not to let them pile up. They didn't exactly have a Sheldon Cooper Roommate Agreement, but still... He added a few items to the grocery list on his phone before he resumed work.

With his deadline looming and nothing yet written, organizing his notes became the priority: the discovery of the article about Alex's disappearance, his trip to Campbell River, his interview with Jameson, his visits to Morgan, and his confrontation with Brad. But none of it answered the question his assignment posed: how was the case resolved? He hypothesized several scenarios, none of which the police had tried, as far as he knew.

His cousin withholding evidence, and the police neglecting to interview Cole that day, were major oversights. It all suggested that Alexis Young's disappearance would remain unsolved unless Jameson found some additional evidence. With his wrists slapped, Oliver wasn't likely to find Alex before his deadline. He'd have to focus on the Renders and try not to insert himself into the narrative.

Oliver glanced at his phone. "Shit." Sid had been sleeping for three hours.

He slipped into the bedroom and touched her arm. "Sid. Are you hungry?"

She stretched and smiled. "Starving." She took his hand and followed him to the table.

Oliver scooped the salad into bowls. "I want you to read my paper. I'm disappointed I didn't solve the case, but I think I've made some observations and posed plausible hypotheses. Would you tell me what you think?"

"Sure. Aren't you going to get that *Observer* editor—Tom what's-his-name—to give you his opinion before you hand it in?"

"Yeah, Tom Foreman. I'm going to email it to him tonight if you think it's ready."

After supper, Oliver paced while Sid read. When she finished, she frowned.

"You didn't like it. What was wrong?"

Sid scrolled through the document. "Wasn't the objective of the assignment to actually find out what happened to Alex?"

"Yes, but that's not possible."

"Not possible in time, you mean? If you're disappointed with it, I can't see how you are going to impress Foreman or your professor."

"It's the best I can do right now. It's been too long. There was no evidence then, and there is less than that now." Oliver hit *send*. "Let's see what Tom thinks."

* * *

THE INCESSANT BUZZING of his phone Tuesday morning jarred him awake. Oliver caught it just before it crept off the night table. "Hello."

"What the hell is this?"

Oliver rubbed his eyes. "Tom?"

"Yes. I wake up to this sorry excuse for a story?"

Oliver lowered his voice as he lifted the covers and slipped out of bed. "It's not meant to be an article for the paper. It's my assignment paper. I just wanted your opinion."

"Well, it sucks."

Oliver glanced back at Sidney when she stirred. He closed the bedroom door without a click as he left the room. "Tell me what you really think."

"The objective was to follow up on a crime for which there was no resolution in the press. Correct?"

"Yes, but—"

"No buts. What was the follow-up? On what did the police base their conclusion? At what point did it become a cold case? I don't see that here. All I see are a lot of libelous accusations disguised as hypotheses. Not only could these two alleged suspects sue you, but the police could lay charges. That's a moot point anyway, because no newspaper editor would print this, ever!"

SIXTEEN

STUNG BY TOM'S REBUKE, Oliver steeled himself for the long haul. After four days and four sleepless nights, he gazed into the bathroom mirror at his bloodshot eyes and scruffy stubble. *It's no use.* He could not put a positive spin on his paper—there would be no resolution to Alex's disappearance. Neither the press nor the police had discovered her whereabouts, and now it was too late. He shaved and dressed, then biked to class to face the music.

He couldn't make eye contact with Professor Keegan as he approached her desk and tossed his paper on the stack. Was it his imagination, or was it thinner than all the others?

Professor Keegan lifted it before the next paper fell on the pile and weighed it in her hand. "By the way you look, this should weigh a lot more, Oliver. Incomplete?"

Oliver moved to stand beside her as the other students filed past. "Yes. Unfortunately. The reporter who initially filed the story on Alexis Young died soon after he retired. I've gone over all of his notes at the paper. I've had Sergeant Jameson reactivate the investigation into her disappearance, but he hasn't learned anything new except what I brought to him. The police never interviewed me at the time. I guess I just chose the wrong crime for this assignment."

"Why would they interview you? How old were you?" She perched on the edge of her desk, pushing the stack of papers behind her. Oliver would have smirked if he wasn't busy lining up his excuses.

"I was eight, and Alex was fifteen. I was probably the last person to see her before she disappeared."

Professor Keegan motioned for Oliver to keep talking.

"When my folks split, and Mom and I moved up to Nanaimo, I was bullied a lot—you know, new kid and all that. Alex rescued me one day after school on the way home. We lived on the same block, so we often walked home together after that. We became friends. I was only eight, and she was fifteen, but I had the biggest crush on her. When she moved away on the last day of school that year, I was brokenhearted. All I knew was that she left and didn't even say goodbye."

"And the police didn't talk to you at all?"

"No." He glanced up to see Alex sitting on the windowsill, thumbing her nose at him. It had been a long time since she'd popped into his head. And it didn't help that Professor Keegan dropped his paper back on the stack and shook her head. "And you didn't mention this to your mother or anyone at the time?"

A chill made Oliver rub his arms. He shook his head. "At that age, I was oblivious to the adult world. I knew nothing except that a very good friend had moved away."

"I can't say I'm not disappointed, Oliver. Perhaps you chose the wrong crime."

"No. The crime is that the case of Alexis Young's disappearance has lain cold for twelve years, making it virtually impossible to solve."

* * *

OLIVER TOOK the stiff wind personally on the bike ride home. He massaged his ego for the rest of the day. Sid ate at the cafeteria instead of coming home before work, leaving Oliver free to wallow in self-pity alone. And he took full advantage of it. The leftover noodles he poked with his chopsticks couldn't arouse his appetite. He scrolled through the channels on TV but then shut it off, slumped on the sofa, and nursed a beer.

He looked around for Alex. Since Sid wasn't home, he risked speaking out loud. "Where are you?"

His computer chair spun around. *I'm here.*

Oliver sighed a deep sigh. "I've let you down, Alex. I don't know where you are. I don't know what happened to you."

I don't think you, like, tried hard enough.

"You've got that right." Oliver rubbed his eyes. "But what can I do? The assignment is over."

Alex hung her head back, looked at the ceiling, and made the chair spin. *I guess that means I'll be right here, with you and Sid, for the rest of your life.*

Oliver's jaw dropped. "No. Can this day get any worse?"

At that moment, his mother's distinctive ringtone startled him. "Mom?"

"Oliver, come to the house right now."

"What's happened?"

"Brad has been assaulted."

"I'm on my way."

* * *

OLIVER WISHED he'd had the car. Gray clouds shrouded Mount Benson, and just as he arrived at his aunt's house, it started to rain.

In the kitchen, his mother sat by the window while Lila paced. Brad's battered face was the first thing Oliver saw when he entered.

"This is all your fault," Brad said.

Oliver pulled up a chair beside his mother and held her hand. "What exactly is my fault?"

"If you hadn't dug up all this shit about Alex, this wouldn't have happened to me." Brad pointed to the stitches near his eye.

Oliver looked at Lila for an explanation. "What happened?"

Lila's arms flailed in exaggerated gestures. "Cole Thomas happened. He did this." She pointed at Brad's various cuts and abrasions.

Oliver leaned toward Brad. "I guess the natural next question would be 'why'?"

Brad began slurring his words. "That prick Jameson had Cole in for questioning, and he figures I told the cop he was at Connie's that day."

"Well, did you?"

Brad shrugged. "Maybe *you* did."

Oliver shook his head. "I didn't know Cole was there until you told me after your interview with Jameson. It had to be you."

"Well, I told Cole that you did, so watch your back, Jack."

Oliver couldn't believe his ears. "Excuse me? Are you saying Cole is going to be after me for something *you* did?"

Brad wobbled on the chair. "I hope so."

Lila kept him from sliding off. "Can't you see he's had a sedative? Olly, help me get him up to bed."

Oliver draped one of Brad's arms around his neck and hoisted him to his feet. "Come on, man. Get your legs under you." The staircase wasn't wide enough for three people, so Oliver muscled the belligerent ingrate upstairs on his own. Lila hovered on the stairs behind them to help him into bed.

Oliver had only a moment with his mother before Lila was back, pointing her finger in his face. "How could you do this to your cousin? Why did you have to dig up this old story? That girl ran away. End of story."

Oliver stood to leave. "I've had enough of this. Your son has lied to Cole, hoping he will do the same to my face. Well, Sergeant Jameson will hear about this, so you can expect him to follow up with Brad. Mom, I'm leaving." He had to get out of there before he said any more.

Lila puffed up like a blowfish. "Lauren, are you going to just sit there and let him talk to me like that?"

"Yes, I am, Lila, because I agree with him."

"Well, maybe you should leave too."

Showing no surprise, Oliver's mother stood and parted the drapes. "It's still raining, Olly. We'll strap your bike in the trunk."

SEVENTEEN

THE DELUGE OVERWHELMED the windshield wipers just as it had that fateful night on the Malahat. Oliver looked at his mother, who was intent on the road. At least she wasn't crying.

At the apartment, he parked his bike in the hall. Kicking off his sodden runners, he took their coats to the bathroom to drip.

He emerged, rubbing his hands and pointing at the sofa. "Have a seat, Mom. With this rain, you would have had to drive me home even if it hadn't come to this."

"Yes, but I knew this day was coming. Brad has been an absolute dolt to live with." She looked around. "Sid is still at work?"

He nodded and checked the time. "She should be home any minute."

And she was. Sid smiled as she stamped her feet and shed her coat like a second skin. Handing it to Oliver, she looked from one to the other. "Hi, Lauren. What brings you out on a night like this?"

Lauren shrugged. "Brad again."

Oliver hung her coat in the bathroom beside his. "I think we all need a hot drink. Tea, anybody?"

Sid plunked down beside Lauren. "Sounds good. What is it this time?"

His mother apprised her of the latest fiasco involving Brad, adding yet another layer of guilt to Oliver's shoulders. "I'm sorry to bring this down on you, Mom."

"Nonsense. This isn't your fault. Brad was an insufferable individual long before you had Alex's case reexamined. He's made no effort to find a job since moving back home. My sister is in for a shock with my moving out."

"I'll bet. Olly and I are happy to put you up until you find a place."

"Thank you, dear. But it will only be for a few days. I knew this day was coming, and this business with Brad was the impetus I needed to say enough is enough. I take possession of my condo next week."

* * *

ALTHOUGH STILL IN A FUNK, Oliver tried to maintain a positive demeanor around his mother that week. She insisted on sleeping on the sofa bed and never once tied up the bathroom. She went to work as usual, shopped for furniture for her condo, and still managed to prepare evening meals for the three of them all that week.

Arriving home after classes, the aroma from the kitchen reminded him how much he had taken his mother for granted in his youth. "It smells wonderful. Thank you, again."

"Small price for putting me up. I have to be at the condo for a delivery shortly. It's all hot. I may be late, so don't wait up." She donned her coat and scooted past Sid in the doorway.

Sid sank into her chair. "I'm going to miss your mother when she moves out."

Oliver leaned over and kissed her. "Me too, but we haven't be able to make love with her sleeping five feet from the bedroom door."

Sid ran her foot up his inseam. "At least I can see her," she said, in an off-hand reference to Alex. "Hang on for a couple of days." She grasped his T-shirt and pulled him down for a passionate tide-me-over kiss.

Oliver groaned, dished out the soup, and placed the sliced baguette on the table. "I regret causing all of this upheaval."

"You regret moving in with me?"

"No, of course not. I guess I'm questioning my motives for opening up this can of worms about Alex's disappearance."

"If I recall, I had to talk you into it."

Oliver rubbed his face with his hands and leaned on his elbows. "I know, but were my motives altruistic—to give closure to others— or did I just want to rid myself of her constant presence in our lives? Either way, I failed."

* * *

THE DAYS TICKED BY. It was June twenty-seventh, the anniversary of Alex's disappearance. Biking home from the library, Oliver stopped at that spot on the trail. If only he had realized the significance of it. If only he had gone with her when she turned toward Connie's Café that day after school. Her leap onto his handlebars was the only thing that got him out of his funk that day.

Oliver looked at the moon through the trees. He had lost track of time at the library, and the gloom between lights mirrored his mood. "Where are you, Alex? Is it possible there could be a clue here that the police overlooked?" He sat, listening to the whispering leaves.

"Still talking to the fairies, you big fuck."

The voice came from behind, before the moon and the park lights went out.

* * *

THE POUNDING in his head was deafening. Faces and voices washed in and out of his consciousness. He was being lifted. His body slid into bright light.

"You're in an ambulance, Oliver. You've got a nasty gash on your head. Can you hear me?"

Could he hear him? He winced. That voice pounded in his head like a jackhammer. Oliver whispered, "My bike."

"Don't worry about it, Oliver. Someone is looking after it for you. Is there someone we should call to come to the hospital?"

"Sid."

"Do you know her number?"

He couldn't think for the searing pain in his head and his eyes.

"Oliver, can you see my hand?"

Spinning light, dizzy, vomit. Sirens drowning voices, questions. Then nothing.

* * *

IN THE LIGHT of day and the comfort of his hospital bed, Oliver examined the bald patch on his skull with a mirror. Laced with black sutures, the laceration looked ugly and angry.

"You are one lucky dude. Can I put on this dressing now?" The massive, blue-gloved hand of Alwyn, his nurse, held the gauze over Oliver's head.

"Sure. What did you call this?"

"It's a brain bruise or contusion."

"So that's lucky?"

"You know it. If you had brain swelling—cerebral edema—they might have had to drill a hole in your skull to relieve the pressure. But let's face it: whoever hit you intended to kill you. That's a whole other level of luck, my man. I'll be back." His fist was twice Oliver's size in the fist bump.

Jameson did a double take as he passed Alwyn in the doorway. "You probably don't need security with him around."

"You haven't found him?"

"Not yet. We're watching Georgia Boyland's place in case either of them shows up there. And I'm interviewing their coworkers."

Oliver winced when he laid his head back on the pillow. "Cole must think Brad told you something about him in connection with Alex's disappearance. Otherwise, why would he attack him too?"

"What? Your cousin, Brad Forrester? Thomas attacked him too? When was this?"

"About a week, ten days ago."

"That would put it right after our interview." Jameson grilled Oliver until he held up his hands in surrender.

"Take pity on an injured man here. I have a brain bruise."

"You probably wouldn't have a brain bruise if you had reported that attack on Brad. Were you poking around in the case again?"

"No, I swear. But those two have got something to hide, or they wouldn't be trying to intimidate me."

"Brad threatened you?"

"Not exactly. But I wasn't going to be the one to report the attack when he had no intention of doing it."

"Look, that knock on the head wasn't intimidation. Thomas meant to kill you. Until we find him, I want you to stay out of dark alleys."

"No problem. I wonder if I didn't have this coming." Oliver wasn't finished with his self-recrimination.

"Don't beat yourself up. Thomas has already done that for you. This may be the proverbial smoking gun. I'm leaving photographs of Cole Thomas and Brad with the staff and security, just in case."

Oliver shook his head and immediately regretted it. "Ow. Brad isn't brave enough to come here or challenge me physically, but you'd better find Cole soon, because I can't take Alwyn home with me."

EIGHTEEN

SID HOVERED over Oliver as he got out of the car at the apartment. She glanced around like a prairie dog.

"Relax, Sid. I don't think Cole is lurking behind the hedge."

His bike stood in its usual place in the hall, and Oliver sighed. "I suppose it's going to be a while before you let me ride again." The precautions from his doctor were depressing.

"You bounced back remarkably, but the doctor said to watch for symptoms for a few weeks." She guided him to the sofa and went back to lock the door. "Feel like a coffee?"

"That'd be great, thanks." Jameson must have told her Cole was still at large. *Dammit, I've brought this to her door.* "I think it's highly unlikely Cole will try a do-over. I mean, the cat is out of the bag, so to speak. He meant to silence me, but I lived to say whodunit. What would be the point?"

"Revenge. If you weren't sure he had something to do with Alex's disappearance before, you certainly are now." Sid set his cup on the coffee table and snuggled against his chest.

Oliver picked up his mug and took a sip. "I'm sorry."

Tears glazed her eyes. "For what?"

"For bringing this down on you." Oliver kissed her.

"Don't be sorry. It was me who talked you into taking on Alex's disappearance as your assignment focus. And maybe I had ulterior motives. Did you ever think of that?"

Oliver turned her face up to look into her eyes. "What motive could you possibly have?"

Sid had that Cheshire-cat grin for dealing with Oliver. "How many years has Alex come between us? You had a crush on her when you were younger. And didn't you tell me she had a crush on you when your age surpassed hers? That was *your* fantasy. It's been a love triangle, Olly. I even had to initiate our friendship with benefits."

Oliver stared across the room at a sullen Alex spinning on his computer chair. He pulled Sid against him. "I had no idea I was so blatantly insensitive and self-absorbed."

Sid snuffled and wrapped her arms around him. "I don't think it was a deliberate effort to shut me out or make me jealous. Other boys, who don't have an Alex, tease girls, pull their hair, or stick anonymous notes in their lockers."

"Boys actually do that?"

"Uh-huh. But girls are a little more subtle."

"Yeah. As I recall, you wanted to cut my grass."

Sid snorted. "You're the one who came up with that, not me. And you tried to blame Alex." Her eyes twinkled like starlight.

"Really?" Oliver kissed her. "I could use a trim."

* * *

AFTER ONLY TWO days of imprisonment, Oliver got paroled. He begged Sid to drop him at the university library while she worked. She conceded, with the proviso that he alert someone if he experienced any symptoms. But Oliver drew the line at wearing a T-shirt that read, *Am I Acting Weird? Call 9-1-1.*

Still sporting an obvious bandage under his cap, he settled at a remote table, opened his laptop, and booted up. His assignment document was pinned to his desktop. He sighed at Alex, who was leaning on the stacks. "What's the point now?"

"Oh, I think there is a valuable point, Oliver."

Startled by the voice, he spun around in his chair. "Professor Keegan."

"Hello, Oliver. I heard about this unfortunate business." She pointed at Oliver's head. "You were the only one who chose a truly unsolved case for this assignment, and since the police have deemed it worthy of reinvestigation, it would be judicious of me to grant you an extension on the deadline and allow you to resubmit."

Wide-eyed, Oliver exhaled abruptly. "I don't know what to say, Professor Keegan, except thank you."

"You're welcome. I'll leave it open-ended for the summer. I hope that gives you enough time. Good luck."

With a nod, she walked away. Oliver glanced around, his eyes gleaming with excitement. Had anyone seen him high-five Alex?

* * *

AS THE DAYS PASSED, so did the risk of Oliver exhibiting latent symptoms from his wound. It had been two weeks, and as cute as it was, Sid wasn't hovering as much. Oliver was restless. A call from Glenda Renders was the perfect excuse to get out of the apartment. At breakfast, he broached the subject with Sid. "I'd like to bring them up to date in person."

Sid topped up their coffee. "What about Jameson's warning?"

"Glenda said Jameson hasn't interviewed them or even told them Alex's case is being reinvestigated. And they certainly haven't told them about what's transpired since."

"Do you intend to tell them about the attacks?"

Oliver poured milk over his corn flakes. "No. I don't want to scare them. I want to let them know the investigation has been reopened, but without giving them false hope. With my wings clipped, I'm not likely to find any new leads—other than this one." Oliver touched the back of his head.

"Well, because of that attack, you've got this assignment extension. If you want to find Alex before the end of the summer, you'll have to be on Jameson's case, so to speak." She got up to put her arms around his neck. "Come on. Call Glenda back, but you'd better get your excuses lined up for Jameson in case he finds out. I'll make a picnic lunch."

* * *

WITH THE WINDOWS DOWN, the wind whipped Oliver's hair and cooled the bald patch that had sprouted an itchy stubble. "Let's pull over and have our lunch on the beach. I want to inhale the sea air and organize my thoughts before we get there."

It wasn't long before Oliver was sitting on a log and burrowing his bare feet in the warm sand. He took a deep breath and, forgetting his wound for a moment, pulled his cap down to shield his eyes from the glare off the waves. "Ow."

Sid handed him a sandwich and a steaming mug of coffee. She looped her arm in his. "Still tender? When they find Cole, I think we'll learn a lot about Alex's disappearance. That goose egg cooked his goose."

She could always see the glass half full and seemed to know when Oliver needed a dose of her optimism. He loved her for it and kissed the top of her head.

"What was that for?"

He smiled. "No reason." They finished their lunch in silence, save for the soaring seagulls and lapping waves.

An hour later, they pulled into the Renders' driveway. Sid thought the house looked sad with its peeling paint and dying plants in the front yard. Oliver wasn't sure he was going to make the inhabitants happy either. However, Glenda greeted them with a smile.

"I was so glad you called back, Oliver. I thought maybe nothing had come of your inquiries. Come in. I've made a cake."

This time, Mr. Render was in a decidedly better mood. He was well-dressed and clean-shaven. The living room was tidy, and the cats had decreased in number.

Oliver sat on the sofa with Sid and commented on Mrs. Render's hair.

"Oh, thank you, Oliver. I just had it done yesterday. Now, can I get you some coffee and cake?"

Remembering the tar they had drunk the last time, they grinned. Of course she could. Mr. Render engaged them in conversation about his new job with a forestry company. "If this proves to be steady work, we may qualify to foster a little one again." He gave them two thumbs up.

Here was a changed man. *Who says a man doesn't define himself by his work?* Oliver felt that way himself, lately.

He had to smirk when Sid insisted Mrs. Render give her the recipe for her delicious chocolate cake. Sid had never made a cake, so this was going to be interesting. With their coffee in hand, Glenda and Rob sat on the edge of their chairs, smiling.

Oliver rubbed his thighs and glanced at Sid for encouragement before explaining that the police had reopened the investigation and reinterviewed the people who had seen Alex the day she disappeared, including him this time. The Renders were hungry for details and seemed comforted when he told them Alex had been a carefree teenager that day, on her way to the coffee shop with her BFF after school. She had stopped to talk to him at the schoolyard gate, wearing that long red scarf she loved so much.

"I'm afraid neither the police nor I have uncovered any new leads. I wish I could say we've made significant progress in the search, but I can't." And, until Cole was in custody, he wasn't about to spark a volley of questions for which he had no answers.

Mrs. Render sat beside Oliver and patted his hand on his knee. "After all this time, we really didn't expect a miracle, but one must always hope, mustn't one?" Oliver didn't feel deserving of all this understanding.

Glenda reached down and took a book from under the coffee table. "Would you like to see the yearbook from that year? You can imagine our surprise when we received it. It's the last reminder we have of Alexis." Glenda opened it and set it on Oliver's knee. "You can see how happy Alex was with her friends."

There was Alex, her long red scarf wound around her neck.

Sid leaned in and touched her picture. "She looks so young here. Back then, we were seven years younger than her. She was almost a woman in our eyes."

Oliver and Sid flipped through the yearbook, recognizing Brad and Cole in the senior-year photos. Then came the photos from games, plays, and debates. After that were the formal photos of the individual graduates in caps and gowns, a group picture of them on the steps of the school, and, to close the book, a collage of photos showing the graduates resplendent in their formal gowns and tuxedos.

Oliver stared in disbelief. Sid gasped. There in a photo, on the arm of Cole Thomas, was Georgia Boyland—her floor-length red gown accessorized with Alex's long red scarf.

With slow, casual movements, Oliver closed the yearbook and slipped it back under the coffee table. Sid was quick on the uptake. She glanced at the ornate analog clock on the living room wall.

"Oh, look. I'm so sorry, Mrs. Render, but we have to get back for an appointment. Thank you so much for the recipe for that scrumptious chocolate cake, but we have to run. Oliver?"

"What? Yes, that's right." He blinked, patted his pockets, and looked left and right. Then, in a moment of clarity, he retrieved the yearbook. "Mrs. Render, could I borrow this for a few days? I promise I'll return it to you in perfect condition."

Glenda agreed without hesitation, lamenting the shortness of their visit as Oliver shuffled toward the door. He could not get out of there fast enough.

Sid drove to a pull-out on the beach. "Let's walk." She always seemed to know when Oliver needed to get those endorphins flowing.

They walked in silence for a while before Oliver spoke. "I'm trying to figure out the sequence of those photo shoots. The class pictures were taken in May sometime, around the same time as ours, right?"

"Yes, but those formal graduation pictures must have been taken at the grad on Saturday evening—after Alex's disappearance late Friday night or early Saturday morning." Sid squeezed his hand. "Olly! Sit down before you fall down."

He heard her voice through the avalanche of thoughts and sat. Sid was checking his pupils while Alex choked him with her scarf.

The words staggered from his throat. "Who... followed you... into the park that day, Alex?"

NINETEEN

JAMESON RETURNED Oliver's call on Monday afternoon. After reaming him out for meddling again, Jameson requested—no, ordered—Oliver to come straight to the detachment and bring the yearbook. As if Oliver would forget it.

When he arrived, Corporal Franks ushered him into the interview room, not Jameson's office. "You been harassing Morgan again?"

"Not a chance, Corporal."

Left alone, Oliver glanced around the utilitarian space. *Not meant for comfort, that's for sure.* He took the yearbook out of his backpack and slid it onto the table. The minutes ticked by. *He's playing with my head.* The scowl on the sergeant's face when he entered the room seemed to confirm his assumption.

Without acknowledging Oliver's presence, Jameson sat opposite him and opened Alex's expanding file to, Oliver assumed, his latest interview with Georgia.

Oliver turned the yearbook to face the sergeant. "Have a look at the pages I've flagged."

Jameson's expression did not change as he examined Alex's class photo. Her best friend was there on the same page. With a raised hand, he cut off Oliver when he tried to point out the "BFF" captions. "Don't speak." He flipped to the senior class page, where Oliver had flagged both Brad and Cole.

This time, Oliver spoke over Jameson's objections. "Obviously, they've changed a lot since then, but you can use this book to find witnesses for that day."

"Oliver. Zip it."

But when Jameson came to the picture of Cole and Georgia, he looked up at Oliver through his eyebrows. "You are absolutely sure this is Alexis Young's scarf?"

"Unequivocally." It was all he could do not to slam his fist on the table. This was bona fide evidence.

"All right, then. Let's get a detailed account of your visit to the Renders on record before I reprimand you for doing just that."

"Ah, Sergeant. You'll give me a reprieve when you get the recipe for Mrs. Render's chocolate cake."

* * *

AN HOUR LATER, Oliver straddled his bike and texted Sid from the detachment steps. She would be getting ready to leave for work.

Oliver: I'm not in jail. J is on board.

Sid: Had to be. Don't wait up. Pub with Miriam—bday.

Oliver: Okay. Don't drive. xox

Sid: xox

That was disappointing. He'd bought a nice bottle of red. As he swung his leg over his bike, he smiled. Her plans wouldn't quash the vindicating satisfaction he was feeling. The bracing evening air made his ride home exhilarating. Its freshness seemed to follow him into the apartment.

He undressed, and stood in front of the refrigerator with the door open. *Beer, or open the wine?* No, he'd save the wine for Sid. *A beer it is.* He fired up his computer to update his notes. Like a concert pianist, he poised his fingers above the keys. He finally felt he would be able to deliver for Professor Keegan and maybe even redeem himself with Tom. Today was progress.

It was challenging to stick to the facts and avoid suspense in reporting his trip to Campbell River and the discovery of Alex's yearbook. Someday, just maybe, the report would be part of a much, much longer feature article. He looked at the time; Sid had already left work. He yawned and headed for bed. Maybe he'd still be awake when she got home. He closed his eyes, smiling at the thought of making love. But at twelve thirty, he awoke to the sound of sirens. No Sid yet. He tried texting but didn't expect she'd hear her phone in the pub. He fell asleep in his ear buds, listening to his playlist. Hours later, when his phone alarm rang, he almost slit his throat ripping them out.

He staggered into the bathroom and threw cold water on his face. *Where is she?* He checked his phone as he undressed to shower. No texts. *Miriam's, maybe? I'll catch her at work.*

Showered and dressed, he texted; eating breakfast. He tried again—and again as he wheeled his bike out the door. *This is stupid. Her phone must be dead.*

When he arrived at VIU, there was her car in the bookstore parking lot, so wherever she'd spent the night, at least she hadn't slept in. *Probably no wine tonight.* Oliver jogged up to the campus bookstore.

Miriam smiled at him as he entered.

"Hi, Miriam, where's Sid? Did she stay at your place last night after the pub?"

Miriam looked puzzled. "No. Didn't she come home?"

Oliver's heart was in his throat. "No. When did you see her last?" He scrolled through his phone. Sid's last text was time-stamped three thirty.

"I guess it was shortly after ten thirty when we left."

"You left with Sid."

"Yes. We only walked together as far as the parking lot, though."

"What? Why?" Oliver's body stiffened.

Miriam looked like she had swallowed a canary. "Well, someone was waiting for her by her car."

Oliver rolled his eyes. "For chrissake, Miriam. Who was it?"

"I don't know. Some guy."

He leaned over the counter into Miriam's space. "What did he look like?"

Miriam backed away. "He was big—over six feet, I'd say. He had dark hair, I think. And a black jacket."

"Did he get out of a vehicle?"

"No, he was just leaning against her car when we walked by, so she told us to go on ahead. Then she said something that was kind of bizarre, because he looked older than her."

"What did she say, Miriam? Spit it out."

As if a light went on, Miriam held up her index finger. "Yes, I think she did mention his name. She said, 'You guys go on ahead. I haven't seen Cole since high-school graduation.' But that doesn't make sense because he was older and…"

Oliver's blood ran cold. He was out the door in an instant, dialing 9-1-1.

* * *

TWO CRUISERS ARRIVED WITHIN MINUTES. Jameson directed his officers to tape off the area around Sid's car as he approached Oliver and Miriam.

"What happened?"

Oliver spoke over Miriam, prompting Jameson to hold up his hand. "One at a time. Oliver?"

He jabbered like a school kid. "Sid didn't come home last night. I thought she slept at Miriam's. Then she wasn't picking up. I thought her phone was dead. So I came here, and that's when Miriam told me— Miriam, tell him." Staving off panic, he paced in a tight circle, interrupting Miriam constantly and prompting Jameson to take him aside.

"Oliver, calm down. I need to hear Miriam." He turned back to her. "Miriam, where exactly was this man standing?"

Jameson stopped her from leaning against Sid's car to demonstrate. As soon as she indicated the spot, he waved in an officer to begin dusting the car.

Oliver paced. "You don't have Cole's fingerprints, do you? Do you?"

Jameson ignored his question and again attempted to calm Oliver. The crowd, attracted by the flashing lights, exacerbated his anxiety. He held his head in both hands. "He's got her. And this," Oliver pointed to the back of his head, "is what he's capable of. You know he was trying to kill me. Oh, god. I can't lose her, Jameson." Oliver slammed his fist against a vehicle in frustration, setting off its alarm.

Jameson motioned to an officer. "Oliver, you're going to sit in the cruiser."

At that moment, the car alarm stopped. A girl in the crowd raised her key fob in the air. "I shut it off, officer. It's my car. Can I take it?"

"Not yet. I'll let you know when."

Oliver sat in the cruiser, texting Sid and sweating. He tried phoning. It rang. Jameson, Miriam, and the officer dusting Sid's car for prints stopped and stared at the car. Heart pounding, Oliver jumped out of the cruiser and charged toward them, his arm extended, his phone like a lance.

Jameson held up his hand like a traffic cop. Without touching the car, he peered through the window. "Oliver, stay back, but don't hang up. I see a handbag on the passenger seat." He walked around to the other side.

"It's in there, Oliver. You can hang up now. Corporal, when you finish dusting this door, let me know. Miriam, I want to speak to campus security."

She pointed to a golf cart approaching from between the buildings. "That's Mark there."

Jameson quizzed the driver about his patrols and VIU's video surveillance before jerking his head toward the security office. "Oliver, come with me."

Inside, Mark sat in front of a bank of screens, rolling from one to the other until he found the recording from the previous night. "The cameras focus on the pay terminals, so some parts of the parking lot are off camera."

"Stop!" Oliver saw Sid, Miriam, and the others step into the frame. Cole was leaning against Sid's car, which was parked five cars from the terminal.

"Go forward slowly," Jameson said as he leaned over Mark's shoulder.

They could see Sid open her car door and throw in her purse. After speaking to Cole for a moment, she waved off Miriam and her friends, who walked out of view. Sid and Cole appeared to talk for a few minutes, both gesturing. Then Cole got in her face, and she backed against her car, shaking her head. Cole looked around and grabbed her by the arm, making Oliver curse and rock from foot to foot.

"He's got her by the arm, Jameson. Shit. He's going to hurt her. Look, look! They're walking away. No no. No no no. They're out of camera range." He reached toward the screen, wanting to swipe them back into view. "Switch cameras. Is there a terminal in that direction?"

Mark shook his head. "But if he took her in a vehicle, maybe there'll be an intersection camera." He looked up at Jameson.

"Why did she go with him?" Oliver stared at the screen, desperation in every word. "Why didn't she scream?"

* * *

AN HOUR LATER, Oliver watched Sid's car disappear on a flatbed tow truck headed for the RCMP impound. Jameson promised he would call as soon as they had it open. Go home, he'd said.

Go home? How could he go home? He stood in the middle of the empty parking lot, unashamedly tearful and rudderless. He lifted his phone to his ear. "Mom?"

* * *

IT TOOK him forty-five minutes to bike to her condo at the north end of town. Twice, honking drivers warned him at intersections. *Pull yourself together, Frampton. Focus.*

His mother greeted him at the door with open arms. He sobbed on her shoulder. "He took her, Mom. Cole has Sid. She walked away with him. Why would she do that?"

"Sit down, Olly. I'll get you some water."

"I could use something stronger."

"You need to keep a clear head, Olly. Your police officer might call."

"I guess so. How about coffee?"

"That I can do. And lunch will be ready soon."

But Oliver couldn't eat. His empty stomach churned and threatened upheaval while he poked the food on his plate with a fork. He couldn't avoid the concerned look on his mother's face.

Four agonizing hours later, his phone rang, and all plausible scenarios clattered into his mind, paralyzing the hand poised above his phone.

"Answer it, Olly."

"Hello."

"It's Jameson. We got Sid's car open. Her phone was down against the passenger door. When did you say she texted you last?"

"Three thirty, when she was leaving the apartment for work."

"Do you know her password?"

"No."

Jameson was silent for a moment. "Her phone must have fallen out of her handbag when she tossed it into the car. That would explain why she didn't answer you all evening."

Oliver rubbed his forehead. "Why? Why didn't I call Miriam then?"

"Had Sid ever stayed over with Miriam before?"

"Once or twice that I can recall."

"So, no alarm bells about this behavior?"

"I guess not, but still…" Oliver's gut wrenched in agony.

"Oliver, quit second-guessing yourself. I want you to go home and stay there. We have a lead. The Aulds Road camera caught four vehicles speeding last night around the right time. One of them was Cole Thomas's truck."

TWENTY

OLIVER WAS guilty of distracted driving again several times on his bike ride home. Once there, he paced like a caged animal between rooms. *Where could he have taken her?*

A crazy thought. Brad had been in Cole's class. He might know something. Oliver glanced at the time: eleven thirty. *Brad should still be up, if he's even at home.*

A groggy voice answered, "What?"

"Brad, it's Oliver. I need your help."

"Fuck off."

"Wait, wait, Brad. Don't hang up. This is serious."

"I couldn't give a shit."

Oliver gritted his teeth. "Brad, Cole has kidnapped Sid."

Brad was silent for a moment. "You're shitting me."

"No! Haven't you seen the news? Cole disappeared after he attacked me—which, by the way, wouldn't have happened if you'd reported your attack. And he kidnapped Sid from the campus parking lot last night. It's on the security video. For fuck's sake, Brad. He might kill her!" Oliver could not prevent his voice from breaking.

"That guy was an asshole. What do you expect me to do about it?"

"You were in the same class. Do you remember where he lived, where he could have taken her? Anything?"

"Well, there was nothing left of the farmhouse after the fire. I don't know where else—"

"What fire? When was this? Where was their farm?"

"Hold on. The fire happened when we were in our senior year, so you do the math. Cole's folks both died in that fire. The cops couldn't pin it on Cole, though."

Oliver hung up and began scouring online obituaries, funeral homes, churches. Keywords: Thomas, fire. And nothing. Not a single article about the fire. He walked away from the computer, got himself a beer, and resumed pacing. How could there be nothing about a fire in which two people died?

Oliver picked up his phone again. This time, the call went to Brad's voice mail. "Brad, I can't find anything about any fire at the Thomas farm. Do you know where it is? I have to find it. Call me back."

It took Brad ten long minutes to return Oliver's call.

"Their last name wasn't Thomas. It was Boisvert, and Cole hated old man Boisvert, his stepfather."

"Boisvert. So that's it." Oliver scribbled the name in his notebook. Then something Alex had said occurred to him.

"Where did Cole go to work out of town during summer break?"

"He worked on his uncle's fishing boat out of Campbell River."

"Thanks, Brad. I appreciate this. I mean it."

"Whatever."

It wasn't long before Oliver had found the late Mrs. Boisvert's obituary and her maiden name: Clement. Brad had gotten the year wrong. Cole's mother had been born and raised in Campbell River. Odd there was no mention of siblings, considering Cole had worked for an uncle there. He looked for the name Clement in Campbell River, on the off chance anyway. Nothing. Back to square one.

Maybe the uncle didn't live in Campbell River; maybe he just moored his boat there. If the uncle was Mrs. Boisvert's brother, the next logical place to look was the commercial vessel directory. In it, he found a boat registered to a Marcus Flores called the *Clementine*. Coincidence? It had a phone number. Should he call? What if Cole was there? Would he put Sid in more danger? He shuddered to think. Maybe the *Clementine* wasn't named after Flores's wife; maybe this wasn't even the uncle.

* * *

AFTER A COUPLE of hours of fitful sleep and long before Jameson got to work, Oliver called the detachment. He needed Sid's car out of the police impound. No, they said, that would not happen. Frustrated, he called his mother.

He struggled to control his voice. "Mom, I need your car. I have to go to Campbell River."

"Of course. Are you going to see Alex's folks again?"

"No, I've got a lead on Cole's uncle, and I'm going to check it out."

"Shouldn't you get the police to follow this up?"

Exasperation snuck into his tone. "Mom, I can't just sit by and do nothing. Cole has Sid, and you know what he's capable of. This is such a long shot, Mom. It could be nothing. I don't even have the name of a person. If I find the uncle, it'll be a hot lead for Jameson."

"Please be careful, Son."

He didn't make her any promises. Luckily, the roads were dry. Oliver biked to his mother's condo in record time and was on the road by eight.

* * *

OLIVER DROVE into the parking lot of the first marina, checking for Cole's truck, though he didn't expect to find it. He walked the wharves, checking the names of all the boats. No

Clementine. There were a few empty slips, however, so he went to the office.

"Excuse me, is the *Clementine* usually berthed here?"

The clerk behind the desk didn't need to check. "Sorry, not here."

The second marina had several empty slips. Again, Cole's truck was not in the lot. The man selling crab right off the dock couldn't have looked more typical if he tried. He wore a black watch cap and a red plaid shirt with suspenders. Oliver almost smiled.

The man noticed. "It's all in presentation, my boy. Are you looking to buy some crab?"

"I wasn't, but maybe I should."

The crabman weighed a couple of excellent crab and handed Oliver the sack.

"Thanks. I'm looking for a particular boat, the *Clementine*. Do you know it?"

"Sure. She's usually in that slip, number thirty-nine, but she's out."

"When will she be back?"

"Depends."

"On what?"

"On her catch. It could be a couple of days. It could be a week."

Oliver tried not to think of Sid on that boat. "Did you see them leave?"

"Them? As far as I know, Flores is the only one on board."

"He wouldn't have taken two or three other people with him?"

"Hell, no. He used to take his nephew when he was young, but he hasn't for years. Funny you should ask. The nephew showed up here yesterday."

Oliver's heart fluttered. "You saw Cole yesterday. Did he have a woman with him?"

"No, and he was some pissed when the *Clementine* was out, I'll tell you."

Oliver twisted the top of the burlap sack. "Could the *Clementine* have come and gone yesterday?"

The crabman shook his head. "Possible, if he was called back, but the *Clementine* wasn't here when I docked last night. You could check with his wife, Bea. The office can give you the number."

Had Cole already killed Sid? Oliver fought to keep his stomach from erupting. The office jotted the Flores address on a scrap of paper, which Oliver jammed into his pocket. He ran to the car and swung the sack of crabs into the trunk.

Behind the wheel, his head spun. He opened the door when his stomach lurched, but he could only dry heave. In his ambivalence, Oliver hoped Cole still had Sid. At least she'd be alive.

It didn't sound like the *Clementine* would accommodate two extra people, let alone three. So… could Cole be at the Flores home? He checked the note in his pocket and headed north. The driveway wound through the woods for a kilometer. If he encountered Cole here, it was a long way back out to the highway. But the thought of Sid in jeopardy kept him going.

He backed out of sight onto the shoulder when the house came into view. Cole's truck could be anywhere. There was little open ground except for a garden. Trees surrounded the house and outbuildings. Slowly, he drove forward, peering into the overgrowth as he went. Every muscle in his body tensed as he drove up to the house. Two mangy dogs circled the car. *Get out now and get my leg chewed off, or wait?* He was relieved, sort of, when a woman stepped onto the front porch and called off the dogs.

Smile, dammit. "Mrs. Flores?" Oliver stepped out, but stood behind the car door.

"Yes, who are you?"

"My name is Oliver Frampton." He looked for any sign of recognition, but her face remained blank.

"What do you want?"

"I was just down at the marina looking for the *Clementine*. I thought maybe Cole had gone fishing with his uncle." Oliver walked a few steps closer.

That got her entire body gyrating. Waving her chubby finger at Oliver, Mrs. Flores descended those steps with the dogs snarling at her side, her ample bosom sliding from side to side across her bouncing belly. "Cole's friend? You get back in your damn car and get the hell off my property. It's the likes of you that turned that kid bad. My poor sister. I'm just glad she's dead and can't see what a criminal he is. Arson, assault, and now kidnapping. Get out!"

Oliver stumbled backward toward the car, his words tumbling out as she loped toward him.

"Mrs. Flores, please. I'm not a friend of Cole's. He's tried to kill me, and now he's kidnapped my girlfriend. He may even have killed her."

Mrs. Flores curled up her index finger and tucked her hand into her pocket.

Oliver stood sideways, pushing the air down with his palms. "Yes. I'm trying to find him, hopefully, before he hurts Sidney."

"She's your girlfriend."

"Yes. Have you seen him?"

Her head rocked with an odd attitude. "I'd call the police."

Oliver went to the trunk and removed the sack of crabs. "Good idea, but be careful."

Presenting them to Mrs. Flores, he said, "The crabman on the docks said Cole had come around looking for your husband yesterday."

Beatrice took the sack but held it well away from her body. "Thank you. I'll have my niece cook them up for supper tonight."

"You're welcome." He opened the car door and turned to look at Mrs. Flores, wondering if he was missing something. "If your husband was out on the *Clementine*, could Cole contact him to come back for him?"

"No. And I'm sure Marcus didn't do that."

"Have you any idea where else he might take her?"

"Besides here? No. I don't think there's anything left of their old place out on Jingle Pot Road." She paused for several seconds. "No. I think this is it."

* * *

OLIVER'S MIND churned as he drove south. The crabman and Mrs. Flores seemed certain Cole was not on the *Clementine. Could Cole have forced his aunt to radio her husband to return during those two days that the crabman was out? I should have left my number.*

He dropped off his mother's car while she was at work and biked home by four. Enough time to call Jameson with an update.

"I just got back from Campbell River."

"Is that what you needed Sid's car for?"

"Yes, but since you wouldn't release it, I borrowed my mother's."

"I was afraid of that. So you're telling me you interfered with our investigation again."

"Not technically—I just expanded it. I got Cole's mother's birth name, Clement, from her obituary, and I learned that she was born in Campbell River. No siblings mentioned, but I thought if I found the uncle, he might know where Cole would hide out. It was such a vague hunch, I thought I'd check it out. It could have been nothing."

"I'm listening."

"I searched licensed fishing vessels and took a chance on the *Clementine*—Clement, Clementine, pretty close. It's normally moored at the CR Marina. That's how I found him. The owner is a Marcus Flores."

"What is the relationship here?"

"Turns out I was right. Mrs. Flores is the aunt. Her sister—Cole's mother, Germaine—died in a house fire along with her common-law husband, Leo Boisvert. Were you stationed here when that happened?"

"No, but when we ran Thomas's fingerprints from Sid's car, they matched his fingerprints from that fire investigation. Cole was the prime suspect, but the evidence just wasn't there."

"There's no doubt they're a match?"

"None. Let's get back to your reckless trip to Campbell River against my specific instructions."

Oliver stifled a smirk. "Right. When I found the marina where Flores berthed the *Clementine*, the guy who sold me the crabs said he'd seen Cole looking for his uncle's boat yesterday. That was the moment I knew Flores was the uncle. The crabman said Cole was angry when he discovered the *Clementine* was out… He also said Cole was alone.

"I drove out to the Flores place from there, and Mrs. Flores came out of the house. She's no fan of Cole's, that's for sure. And she didn't think her husband would ever take Cole on the *Clementine* again, let alone with a girl tagging along. You know, she never mentioned a radio, and I never thought of it until after I left."

Jameson seemed to have gotten over being angry with Oliver. "The *Clementine* would have a radio."

"Okay. Why didn't she mention it? Sergeant, I think he's still in the area, but where is Sid when he's alone on the dock? What has he done with her? I keep asking myself, why?" Oliver lost his voice.

"Why did he kidnap Sid? It may have been without premeditation and now he needs her to bargain his way out of this mess. But why would he want to get on that boat?"

Oliver struggled to compose himself. "Maybe we're asking the wrong question. Maybe it's *where*. Where could the boat take him to hide out? A fish camp somewhere in the islands?"

"Possible. This warrants further investigation. The address and phone number for Flores?"

Oliver gave Jameson lengthy directions to the Flores place, as well as a description of the crab vendor and the *Clementine* berth number.

"I suppose if I give you another warning, you'll just ignore it."

"Jameson, I can't sit at home and do nothing, not knowing if Sidney is hurt or—"

"Oliver, there has been no hard evidence of Cole's involvement in Alexis's disappearance. His kidnapping of Sidney suggests he thinks we're getting close to that proof, whatever it is. He's desperate, so he'll be taking excellent care of Sid, his bargaining chip."

TWENTY-ONE

OLIVER WOKE UP SWEATING, his pulse racing. "Sid!" His voice echoed in his skull. *Where has he taken her? She can't be dead; she just can't be.* Mechanically, he stripped off his briefs and turned on the shower. There, he could deny his tears.

Mid-shave, Oliver nicked his chin. "Ow!" He glared with wide eyes at his bleeding chin, which got him thinking about blood, and then death.

"There must have been blood at the scene when Teddy died. I just didn't see it in the darkness. So when did Teddy imprint?"

He answered his reflection. "When I thought we were going to plunge off a cliff and die? No." He shook his head. "When Teddy lay there in the rain, staring at me, as helpless and friendless as I felt that night. That was the moment."

Oliver rinsed his razor and shook it at the mirror. "And Alex?" He stuck out his chin to shave his neck—a difficult thing to do when you're talking to yourself. "Could she have died in the park that night?" He stopped talking before he could inadvertently slit his own throat. They hadn't found her body in the park. *Where else did they search?* Oliver took another stroke under his chin and rinsed his razor. He wiped the last bit of shaving cream from his face and leaned on the sink.

He scowled at the mirror. "If this gut-wrenching mental anguish is the trigger, why isn't Sid sitting on the edge of the tub watching me shave right now?"

He knew in his heart that, at eight years old, he'd had no reasonable expectation of ever seeing Teddy or Alex again—whereas the man in the mirror desperately needed to believe he'd find Sid alive.

"I've got to get Jameson to Campbell River." Oliver quickly dressed and grabbed his cell phone from the charger on his desk.

He glanced at Alex sitting at Sid's easel staring at a blank canvas. "I am so sorry, Alex. I promise I will find your killer, but first I have to find Cole and bring Sid home."

Alex nodded.

* * *

"YOU HAVE REACHED Sergeant Jameson's voice mail. If this is an emergency, hang up and dial 9-1-1. Otherwise, please leave a detailed message."

Oliver's hands trembled. "Sergeant, I believe Alex was killed in the park that night; she was not a runaway. We need to talk. Call me ASAP."

Oliver felt like he had just brought down a moose, and he was ravenous. He cracked eggs and fried bacon. A few tomato slices on the side and he dug in. Between mouthfuls, he tapped his phone, reassuring himself it was on and fully charged. Even so, when it rang, he almost choked. "Hell—" He cleared his throat. "Hello."

"What are you talking about, Oliver?"

"It's hard to explain, and a long story. Can I come to your office?"

"I thought I'd already convinced you that Cole needs Sid alive. But if you have new information, you'd better come in."

Oliver gulped the last of his coffee and was off. Twenty minutes later, he sat in Jameson's office, trying to explain what an imprinted memory was.

"You've heard stories of ducks following people after they hatch? Well, this is sort of like that."

Jameson crossed his arms across his chest. "There'd better be a good reason we're talking about ducks."

Oliver held his palms out. "Just hear me out, and you'll understand why I believe Alex was killed in the park that night." He sat across from Jameson and leaned over the table. "It all began on my eighth birthday." Jameson listened without interruption to Oliver's description of the accident and how Teddy became his imaginary friend, and then his friendship with Alex and the events of that last day of school in 2009, when Alex became his second imaginary friend.

Jameson looked askance at Oliver. "And you talk to them?"

"Yes. It has been the bane of my existence for twelve years." Oliver paced as he described the bullying and Cole's role in it, his therapy sessions with Christine Hunter, his coping mechanisms, and the range of emotions he felt as the years ticked by.

Jameson leaned back. "What did these imprints tell you?"

Oliver scowled and rocked his head from side to side. "You don't understand. They are imaginary. They tell me nothing I don't already know. It was like arguing with myself. They were called my imaginary friends when I was young. I guess they are kind of alter egos. Do you have any kids, Sergeant?"

"Not yet."

"Well, imagine a little girl at a small table having a tea party with her favorite stuffies or empty chairs. She talks to them, or pretends to talk to someone who isn't there. Carries on conversations by putting words in their mouths. Is she nuts? No."

Jameson nodded in agreement.

Oliver threw up his hands. "There you go. The only difference is, my imaginary friends are—were—real people."

"You still talk to these imaginary friends, as you call them?"

"Not very often in the last few years, but when I found that article about Alex, my coping skills went out the window."

"What changed things this morning?"

"I cut myself shaving." Oliver pointed to his chin. "And it suddenly hit me—about the moment I first imagined Alex. According to all of your interviews, Alex was last seen entering the park, right?"

Jameson nodded.

"When I biked through the park that evening, it was after nine, and I was very upset about Alex leaving. I know the exact spot where she hopped onto my handlebars."

"You thought she had just died?"

Oliver frowned. "No. I didn't even realize she was imaginary until I got home, and there she was. Assuming she had just moved to Campbell River, it never occurred to me she might be dead until I read that article twelve years later." Oliver pointed at the closed file in front of Jameson.

"And you don't remember seeing anything unusual in the park that day?"

"You mean other than a figment of my eight-year-old imagination jumping out of the bushes and scaring the shit out of me?"

"I see your point." Jameson sat, deep in thought, while Oliver paced in small circles.

"Jameson, this morning I promised Alex I'd find her killer, but first we have to find Cole and rescue Sid. I just know she's alive. I know it." Oliver suppressed the panic that lurked beneath the surface. "She has to be."

* * *

JAMESON LEFT the interview room without a word, leaving Oliver to stew.

He thinks I'm nuts. This was a bad idea. I should be out there looking for Cole myself.

When Jameson returned with two cups of coffee, Oliver wrung his hands and jabbed the table with his index finger. "I hope you're not stalling—waiting for the ambulance to arrive with a straitjacket."

Jameson held up his palms to Oliver. "No. I believe you, and I understand your frustration, but we need to begin with what we know, and that is here. Georgia has turned up. One of my officers is bringing her in. I think she can provide credible leads to Cole's whereabouts and, if we're lucky, give us some idea of his state of mind when he kidnapped Sid."

Oliver slammed his fist on the table. "Fine. Fine. Ask her what we already know. He's somewhere near Campbell River or the property on Jingle Pot Road. You know they suspected him of arson and manslaughter when his folks died in the fire. And the reason he kidnapped Sid? Not just for revenge. She's a hostage. The only question is, where is he holding her? We have to get back up to Campbell River."

Jameson was the consummate police officer. "I'm on your side, Oliver, but we are going to interview Georgia before we take off in all directions. Because you were a witness, I want you to listen in on the interview. All right?" All Oliver could do was nod.

Jameson stood and headed for the door. "Come with me." He escorted Oliver to the CCVE terminal. "Here's a headset. When I wrap it up in there, Corporal Burns here will take you back to my office. Understood?"

"Got it." Relieved and eager, Oliver donned the headset and sat down to watch and listen with the corporal.

Jameson took with him the Alexis Young file and a thinner one. He had a very smooth entrance that had made Oliver squeamish the first time Jameson interviewed him, and it looked like it was having the same effect on Georgia. Or maybe it was just her conscience making her shift uncomfortably in her chair.

Corporal Burns nodded toward the terminal. "You know this woman?" he asked Oliver.

"Yes, she was the best friend of Alexis Young twelve years ago when Alex disappeared."

"What's your interest in this cold case?"

"I was one of the last people to see Alex alive." Oliver tapped his earphones. He wanted to listen to Jameson.

After Jameson cautioned Georgia, he opened Alex's file. "Ms. Boyland. Have you heard from Cole Thomas since our last interview?"

"No. I think he's gone fishing."

"Fishing."

"Yes, he has an uncle in Campbell River who has a boat."

That part checked out, but Jameson didn't let on.

"Georgia, what does Cole drive?"

"A black Dodge Ram. Why?"

"He went through a red light last Monday night."

"What's that got to do with me?"

"Well, Georgia, he can't be fishing with an uncle if he's running red lights in Nanaimo. Where is he?"

"I don't know. He'll show up. It's a goddamn ticket, for chrissake."

"Not exactly. You and Cole were at Connie's Café the afternoon that Alexis Young disappeared."

"So we're back to that again, are we? I told you that already."

"Well, here's the thing, Georgia: your stories don't jibe with the other witnesses, so we're going to go over it one more time."

Jameson kept her off-balance and caught her contradicting herself from previous statements. After forty-five minutes, she was eyeing the door, visibly defiant. She slouched in her chair and crossed her arms, her answers reduced to yes and no.

"Georgia, when you left Connie's, Cole went in the opposite direction, and he normally takes the trail through the park, doesn't he?"

"Yes, but so does Brad. And he left before me. I think he did it. Alex teased him. It made him mad because she wouldn't go out with him."

"*What* exactly do you think Brad did?"

Georgia backpedaled. "Maybe he... he ran away with her or something and then came back."

Jameson set a copy of Cole's graduation picture in front of her.

Georgia picked it up and smirked. "Alex was sure pissed when Cole asked me to his grad."

"You look lovely, Georgia. Where did you buy your gown?"

"We went over to Vancouver especially."

Jameson pointed to the scarf. "That scarf looks very much like this one." He flipped to Alex's class photo. "Did that scarf come with the dress?"

Georgia sat, staring with her mouth open.

Jameson prodded her. "Georgia? Did that scarf come with the dress?"

"Yes."

"That is a lie, Georgia. That is Alex's scarf. The same scarf she was wearing on the day she disappeared. How did you get it? I think you followed her into the park the day before this picture was taken —the day she disappeared—and killed her."

Oliver turned away from the terminal. "Damn." There was Alex, perched on a desk, looking more upset than he had ever seen her.

Georgia shouted in Jameson's face. "No!"

"You killed her because you were Cole's second choice."

"No!"

"Alex snubbed Cole, and you were the rebound relationship."

"No!" Georgia got up and backed away from the table.

"Sit down, Ms. Boyland." She hesitated in defiance before sitting.

"Did Cole give you that scarf?"

"No!"

"Then how did you get it?"

"She— she gave it to me at Connie's when we said goodbye."

"Do you want to try again, Georgia?"

"What does it matter if Cole gave it to me? Doesn't mean he killed Alex."

Oliver gasped. A chill made him shiver.

Burns nodded. "She's digging a hole."

Jameson pressed on. "Why do you think Alex is dead? It says in this police report she ran away."

Georgia snuffled. "You're confusing me. Trying to make me say stuff. Cole always liked me best. He had no reason to kill her. She ran away, just like it says. I only thought she might be dead because that little shit, Olly, stirred things up again."

Jameson stared at her for a moment. "I think Cole had something to do with Alex's disappearance, and you are covering for him. That would make you an accomplice. Where is he, Georgia?"

"I don't know. I don't know."

"If he's done nothing wrong, why did he kidnap Sidney Wheeler?"

Georgia's eyes bulged. "What?"

* * *

NOW, almost seventy-two hours after Sid had walked out of that video with Cole, the burning question still haunted Oliver. Why had she gone with him so willingly? Oliver wrestled with the question as he biked home. Working on the assignment was out of the question. He needed to do some stress eating. He stared at the pizza box in the fridge. Good enough. As he scarfed down a cold slice, his phone chirped.

It was Gil Wheeler, Sid's itinerant father.

"Hello, Gil... Yes, Staff Sergeant Jameson is handling the case... How could I get in touch with you? Did you leave any contact information with your daughter? No... Well, I'm sorry you feel that way, but now that you have met Sergeant Jameson, I'm sure he'll keep you informed... And goodbye to you too."

Oliver couldn't stop trembling. "Son of a—" His phone chirped in his hand again.

This time, it was his mother.

"Nothing yet, Mom. I just got back from the police station. They interviewed Georgia again. She seemed genuinely surprised to hear that Cole had kidnapped Sid, and she was definitely hiding something about Cole. Jameson will be watching her, I'm sure."

"That's it?"

"Well, no. Cole was caught on a red-light camera at Aulds Road, so he was heading north, and Georgia claimed he might have gone fishing with an uncle in Campbell River. That checks out with what I discovered yesterday."

"Have they searched the place on Jingle Pot Road?"

"They were watching it before Sid..." He fought the feeling of being strangled. "Before Sid was taken, but there wasn't anything. Cole's been crashing at Georgia's, so I'm sure they'll get a search warrant for her place now. She was cunning enough not to bring her phone to the police station today, which gave Jameson cause, I think."

After extracting a promise from Oliver to keep her updated, Lauren said goodbye. She didn't want to tie up his phone. Oliver grinned. *She still doesn't get call-waiting.* It got him thinking about Georgia's phone. If there were calls from Cole on it, maybe he'd called Sid as well to arrange the meeting. *But then why didn't she tell me? Right. Her phone dropped out of her purse in the car beforehand.*

He vowed he would share all his passwords with her in the future.

"Hmm." *Passwords.*

What did she always say? *Before you can get into my phone, get into my heart.* "That's it!"

Within seconds, he had Jameson on the phone. "I think I know Sid's phone password."

"Excellent. Hang on. I'll get it."

Oliver paced.

"Okay. Shoot."

"Do you see a grid of dots or a text box?"

"Dots."

"Okay. Draw a heart."

"What?"

"Connect the dots to make a heart."

"Hang on." Another interminable wait on hold.

"We're in. Just a minute... Yes, there's a text."

"Well?" Oliver practically choked his phone.

"It says, 'I know who killed Alex, and I can prove it. Meet me at your car.'"

Oliver looked at the ceiling and swallowed hard. "But since her phone was in her car, not her purse, she didn't reply."

"Right. Come down and look at that surveillance video again. There must be something, some gesture you might recognize that will tell us why she went with him willingly. Corporal Burns will set it up for you."

"Where will you be?"

"Getting a search warrant for Georgia's place."

TWENTY-TWO

BACK AT THE DETACHMENT, Corporal Burns fast-forwarded the video of the parking lot.

Half rising from his seat, Oliver pointed at the screen. "Stop. There. They are just coming into view."

Burns tsked. "That guy is staying out of sight until she's right there at the back of the car."

"Right. Sid doesn't see him. She hesitates right there."

"Okay, there, she's waving off the others. Who are they?" Burns asked.

"They work with Sid in the campus bookstore. Okay, she opens the car door and throws her purse in, but right there. Look. She puts her foot in and stops. He's saying something. Right there. He's put his hand on her arm."

Burns nodded. "Right, he's squeezing her arm. She's looking down at his hand."

Oliver jumped up, his heart racing. "Sid, Sid. Why aren't you screaming?"

"It all depends on what he's saying to her. It could be a threat, or he may be telling her something that she can't verify, or luring her away from the surveillance cameras."

Oliver squeezed his head to keep it from exploding. "I don't get it. She closes the car door, but I don't see her lock it. Did you?"

Burns shook his head, leaned back in his chair, crossed his arms, and glared at Sid's car alone in the parking lot. "No. It was locked the next morning. She wouldn't lock it if she was coming right back. Something must have happened at his truck. Thomas had to have locked it after he took her hostage. That takes forethought. Premeditation."

* * *

CORPORAL BURNS' phone rang. It was Jameson.

"Yes, he's still here... Right away... The address? ... On our way." He hung up. "Come on, Frampton. Jameson has something for you at Boyland's."

"Me? What could... Is Sid there? Is she okay?"

"He didn't say," was all Oliver could get out of the tight-lipped corporal. Georgia's apartment was only five blocks from the detachment, but no amount of leaning forward in the back seat would get them there any faster. The officer at the door stepped aside for them.

Jameson stood in the middle of a ransacked room. "There you are."

Oliver glanced around at the blood on the floor, his heart in his throat. "Sid? Georgia?"

"I don't know. Watch your step. There's some blood over here, drops, but not a lot. Whoever was injured here either walked out or was carried."

Oliver kneeled by the blood. He felt sick.

"Don't tell me you feel something? Or see someone?"

"What?" Oliver stood up. "Don't be ridiculous."

"Well, you've convinced me of some pretty weird stuff, Oliver. I'm giving you the benefit of the doubt."

"Is this why you brought me here? To see if I could conjure up some ghost or something?"

"Take it easy, Oliver. If Thomas left the parking lot with Sid and headed north, why would he come back here? I can't see why he would bring Sid here after successfully getting her out of town. Do you see any sign of Sid at all? Look carefully. She may have left you some clue we wouldn't recognize."

Oliver looked under the scattered papers, magazines, cushions, and clothes. Nothing. He checked the cracks of the couch, knowing full well if Sid was going to leave him a clue, it would be in plain sight.

Jameson followed him around. "It's obvious Cole was living here. So why toss the place... unless he was looking for Georgia's phone?"

Oliver cocked his head to the side. "Why don't you call it?"

Jameson almost rolled his eyes as he took out his phone. "You don't think he would have thought of that?"

Oliver shrugged. "Georgia might have told him you took it." Oliver tried to imagine the confrontation with Cole.

Jameson called her number. "Everybody, be quiet."

Nothing. No ring. Oliver held his finger to his lips and tip-toed around the blood and clutter. He opened doors as he went down the hall and listened. When he opened a linen closet, he heard a faint buzz. He slipped his hands among the blankets, sheets, and towels. The buzz got louder and louder as he pulled out the thick towels one by one until the phone fell out on the floor.

With one click, he could tell there was no password. "We're in luck." He held it so Jameson and Burns could see.

Cole: cops there?

Georgia: no. use back way?

Cole: ok, u tell cops?

Georgia: no. UFI! Y Sid?

Cole: leverage

Georgia: on u this time

The three men exchanged grim looks.

Oliver picked up a hairbrush by the bristles. "Do we have Georgia's DNA?"

"Not yet." Jameson opened an evidence bag and slipped in the brush, then opened another for Georgia's phone.

Burns kneeled down by the pool of blood to collect a sample. "If Cole thinks we have the phone and have read this, then Boyland's life is not worth shit."

* * *

BURNS DROVE Oliver back to the detachment. It was a sober bike ride home from there that evening, and he was no closer to finding Sid. Oliver parked his bike in the hall and kicked off his shoes. He grabbed the remote and turned up the volume for the news. Jameson was being interviewed. At the mention of Cole Thomas's name, Oliver squeezed the remote so hard the back popped off and the batteries fell out. "Shit."

The photo from the red-light camera of Cole's truck came up on the screen, along with Cole's face and Georgia's—both retrieved from her phone. "Georgia Boyland is also sought for questioning."

Oliver retrieved the batteries that had rolled under the sofa. Finding Georgia's phone had been a real coup for him. Jameson had been impressed and maybe even a little embarrassed, but that didn't mean he was going to call him in again. Oliver's phone was charging just in case.

He lowered enough pasta into the boiling water for two. On edge with worry about Sid and the whole cockeyed investigation, he stirred too vigorously and splashed his hand. "Shit." His first thought was "cold water." Standing there, leaning on the sink, he couldn't hold back a wracking sob. *Sid.*

Recovering his composure, he wondered what else could go wrong. He gazed at the excess food he had prepared. Of course, there would be leftover salmon sauce and pasta—Sid wasn't here. He ate in silence, the television muted, his thoughts rambling. Then he shoved his empty plate across the table and leaned forward with his head in his hands.

Oliver knew full well why Cole had taken Sid. *It's my fault.*

Skirting the edge of self-control, he needed to do something. But what?

He needed to connect with the past. Walk the walk. Talk the talk, especially with the people who were there. Not in the parking lot at VIU, but at Connie's Café, where Georgia and Cole had been that day twelve years before. Something had happened back then that made Georgia text "on u this time."

He left the dishes in the sink.

* * *

CONNIE'S HAD SEEN a few changes over the years. New benches and chairs that didn't dig holes in the floor. And gone were the days of black coffee with cream or sugar. The espresso machine churned out any concoction one could imagine. The only thing that hadn't changed was Connie herself. She was the same sociable, motherly type who knew the name of every kid who'd ever hung out there after school.

Oliver slid into an empty booth. "Hi, Connie. I'll have a cappuccino, please." He glanced around. A couple chatted in the booth at the end, and a man in the next booth was reading a paper and nursing his coffee. "Have you got time to talk?"

"Sure, Olly. But come over to the counter."

The stools were no longer the old swivel style bolted to the floor, but sleek and modern. Connie's had lost its retro vibe.

"You've seen the news lately?" he asked.

"Yes, Olly. I'm so sorry. Sidney was a sweet girl. You've been chums for a long time, haven't you?"

"Yes. And now Sid is a sweet woman. We're living together. I'm going out of my mind." He pointed to his head. "Cole tried to kill me, and now he's taken Sid." His voice cracked.

Connie set the cappuccino in front of Oliver. She'd drawn a heart in the foam. "Tell me what happened. Why did he do this?"

Two coffees and a piece of bumbleberry pie later, Oliver had filled her in on all that he knew, from the reopening of Alex's case to Sid's abduction and Georgia's suspicious disappearance.

Oliver pressed his fork into the few remaining crumbs on the plate. "You know I wasn't here the day Alex disappeared, but I met her at the back gate. Normally we'd walk home together, but that day, she and Georgia were going to meet friends here to say good-bye. Since she was leaving for Campbell River in the morning, Alex had resigned herself to the fact that Cole was taking Georgia to grad."

"Yes, I remember that day. And I've had to retell my recollections to the police many times—then and now."

Oliver spun around on his stool and pointed out the window to the parking lot. "You saw the altercation between Scott Morgan and Alex through that window, right?"

"Yes. At first, I heard it. Cole had just come in to use the bath-room when I heard a car door slam. I looked up and saw Morgan charging, if you could call it that, on crutches to where Alex was standing. Of course, I didn't know who it was then. The door closed, and I continued to watch what was going on. I could tell he was yelling, but when he flipped her scarf in her face and grabbed her arm, I was out there in a second. I yelled at him, saying I had called the police. Brad and Georgia were yelling at him, too. I wasn't about to feel sorry for him just because he was on crutches. He flipped me the finger, got in his car, and drove away."

"Why do you suppose Alex left before the police got here?"

"She called out that she knew him and deserved it. She asked me not to call the police, but I already had. That seemed to upset her more than the incident. I came back inside—I had customers. The last I saw of Alex, she was having an animated conversation with Georgia. By the time Cole went back outside, Alex had left."

"What happened when the police arrived?"

"They came in first, and I told them to go back outside and talk to Georgia and Brad before they left. I didn't see Cole outside when they went out."

"You didn't see Cole leave?"

"No. But he hadn't seen the altercation anyway. He was in the bathroom. So it didn't matter much."

Oliver cupped his coffee mug in both hands. "I wonder if he left after Alex did and before the police even arrived."

"I suppose that's possible. Maybe I was serving. I don't remember seeing him come out of the bathroom."

Oliver looked toward the hall that led to the bathroom, gauging its proximity to the front door and the window to the parking lot.

"Do you remember Cole coming in here with Georgia after that weekend?"

"Oh, yes, they were thick as thieves after that. Well, until he went fishing with his uncle for the summer. I could see Georgia had a thing for Cole even when he was after Alex. Kids have raging hormones they can't control at that age."

"Tell me about it." Oliver couldn't prevent his blush. "Could I have another piece of that pie, Connie?" This was more information than he ever got from Jameson, and Oliver wanted her to keep talking.

"Never could fill you up, Olly."

"Thanks, Connie. You know, Cole's truck was last seen heading up island. We think he had Sid with him. But Georgia's disappeared too, so we think he came back for her. Not sure why... The crabman at the marina in Campbell River saw him before Georgia disappeared, but no one, including his aunt, has seen him since. We know he has Sid, but we don't know where." Oliver gripped his fork like an ice pick.

Connie poured herself a cup of coffee. "That boy was always troubled, but he became quite sullen after the fire. The police couldn't prove he started it, but suspicion hung over his head after that. He became even more bitter and aggressive."

"Don't I know it. It was Alex who defended me back then. She really shamed him sometimes. Even after he graduated, he bullied me. He always had a chip on his shoulder. That's why I think he's responsible, somehow, for Alex's disappearance." Oliver pushed his empty plate away. "And now Sid... and maybe Georgia."

TWENTY-THREE

UNABLE TO SLEEP THAT NIGHT, Oliver tossed and turned for hours. The moon shone through the vertical blinds, casting shadows like prison bars across the room. *Prison. That's where Cole should be.* He got up and opened the window. The cool night air filled his lungs.

He glanced at his phone. Four thirty. Oliver dressed and made himself a bacon-and-eggs breakfast. Ever since he'd heard about the Clement fire, he'd wondered what had happened to Cole after that. He couldn't have gone into foster care at eighteen. And his aunt definitely hadn't taken him in, so maybe he'd been homeless? When did he hook up with Georgia?

The moon was still bright in the sky—a perfect time to bike out to the old Clement place. As he left the apartment, he held his bike against his thigh and turned the key. *Does Sid have her key?* No, it was in her purse, in evidence. He hesitated to take the key from the lock. It was a stupid impulse. She wasn't coming home.

On the road, Oliver pushed himself until his lungs burned. Lights popped on in homes as people rose to face the day. He wondered how many of them would go about their day gripped in fear as he was. *How do they do it?* Dogs barked, and the streetlights went out.

He stopped at the top of a rise and checked the map on his phone. The side road said *No Exit*. This was it. The houses grew farther and farther apart until he came to open fields. At the end of the road was an overgrowth of trees around the perimeter of a yard —a yard that was empty save for a dilapidated shed. Far beyond the trees, the roof of a barn sagged in the middle like a swayback horse. The place was deathly quiet except for the slow crunch of gravel beneath his tires.

Shrubs that had grown in the shelter of eaves now flourished above the house foundation. Not a stick remained of the original structure. Within the walls of the foundation, fixtures lay charred beyond recognition in the overgrown grass. The fire must have raged with no alarm sounding or any attempt to fight it. For a moment, he almost felt sorry for Cole, who'd lost his mother and stepfather in such a horrific way. He wondered where Cole could have been that night—a school night.

Oliver walked his bike over to the shed. The crossbar lifted easily from its brackets, but the door resisted, creaking on rusty hinges. Dust rose in the early-morning light, revealing an old riding lawnmower surrounded by rusted gardening tools and flowerpots filled with cobwebs. He left it all undisturbed.

Leaving his bike against the shed, he walked with long strides through the weeds to the barn. One door hung from a hinge, making no attempt to keep him out. He stood inside, waiting for his eyes to adjust to the dim light. Birds fluttered in and out through a gaping hole in the roof while mice scurried along the walls into cracks.

Odd, he thought, that while they had left equipment outside to rust and decay, someone had moved the stock. Did Beatrice Flores look after her sister's estate but not take in Cole? Oliver walked the length of the barn, checking the stalls on either side, some with names. He wondered who Colette was. A favorite milk cow, perhaps?

When he opened the last stall, something looked off. The hay looked recently disturbed, and a horse blanket lay crumpled in the corner. His heart leaped into his throat when he dragged it a few feet out with his heel. Backing out of the stall, he fumbled with his phone.

* * *

JAMESON'S VOICE mail could not have been more indifferent. Oliver hung up and dialed 9-1-1. "Police. Specifically Sergeant Jameson. It's urgent."

Oliver walked out into the open, worried that he had already disturbed a crime scene.

"Sergeant Jameson."

"It's Oliver. I'm out at the Clement property, and I think I've found fresh blood in the barn."

"Get out of there."

"I am out. I think you'd better get out here."

"We were just leaving for Campbell River, but we'll divert. Be there in twenty minutes. Meet us on the road."

Oliver tried to retrace his steps through the weeds back to the farmyard, wondering if he'd disturbed someone else's. As he stood in the driveway, waiting, his mouth felt dry but his hands clammy. He took a bottle of water from his backpack and drained it. In the distance, he saw flashing lights. The thought of Sid bleeding in that barn made Oliver lean into the weeds and retch just as the cruiser came to a stop.

Jameson donned his cap as he approached him. "Are you okay?"

"Not really."

"Take it easy. When you're ready, walk me through it."

Oliver rested with his hands on his knees before nodding to Jameson.

The two Mounties scanned the ground ahead of them as they walked.

"I stood here and just looked at how overgrown the foundation was. I walked over to this shed, took the crossbar off, looked inside, put the crossbar back, and left my bike here."

Jameson stopped him every few feet to examine the ground as he retraced his steps to the barn. There were signs of a vehicle having disturbed the grass, but the thatch was too thick for tire tracks. They examined the barn door as they stepped through. Now midmorning, sunlight streamed through the roof and numerous broken wall boards.

Bits of straw littered the floor, making Oliver's scuff marks discernible as they walked toward the far end.

Oliver said, "I was just looking in the stalls, wondering what happened to the stock, when I came to the last one and discovered this."

Jameson gave Oliver a steely glare. "You went in there."

"Yes, and I pulled that horse blanket out of the corner with my heel."

"Dammit, Frampton."

"I'm sorry. As soon as I saw the blood, I backed out."

Neither Jameson nor Burns entered the stall, but they glanced around for any other disturbance in the straw dust. Jameson pointed toward the back doors.

"There. Burns, photograph." His finger made a large circle in the air. "Oliver, are you absolutely sure you did not go near those doors?"

"Yes, absolutely." He stared at a patch of oil on the floor.

When Burns was satisfied with his images, he nodded. Jameson lifted the latch holding the doors together and pushed. As they stepped out into the bright sunlight, he said, "No further."

An arc of flattened grass extended behind each door. A vehicle could have easily slipped into the barn. Sure enough, two swaths of flattened vegetation led away from the back of the barn: one along the outside of the tree line surrounding the farmyard to the gravel driveway, and the other across a field toward a densely wooded area.

Jameson held his phone to his ear. "We need a police service dog."

* * *

NOT WASTING A MINUTE, Jameson gave orders to Burns as they walked back to the cruiser. It was all a blur to Oliver. His next bottle of water stayed down, barely. *Please let this be animal blood.* He couldn't imagine the alternative.

Jameson debriefed Constable Cheswick when he arrived with the police service dog. Oscar sat dutifully at heel, watching his handler's every gesture.

They were about to set off for the barn when Jameson held his arms out. "You'd better stay here, Oliver."

When Oliver tried to dodge past him, Jameson took him by the shoulders. "Look. We don't know what we're looking at here."

"You mean *who!* Jameson, you're going to have to handcuff me to the gate to keep me away. I swear I'll stay out of the way."

"And if it's Sid?"

"It won't be, I know." Oliver's tone waffled between hope and certainty.

Jameson stuck his finger in Oliver's face. "Behind me. If I see you out of the corner of my eye, I'll tell Burns to shoot you."

Burns shook his head and followed, carrying two shovels.

When Cheswick gave Oscar the scent on the horse blanket in the end stall, the dog went to work. As predicted, Oscar led them across the field to the woods. The thick brush made it difficult to follow. They first had to navigate between blackberry bushes that snagged their pant legs and sleeves. Oscar stopped and sat behind an uprooted tree. The earth all around it had been disturbed, but there was no depression where the roots had been.

Jameson pushed Oliver back, forcing him to sit on a stump. Oliver's ears rang with the sound of shovels ramming into the ground. Each blade sliced through his heart. The earth was loose and, far too soon, they found something. Someone. Jameson pointed a warning finger at him before carefully brushing dirt from the body's face.

It was Georgia. Oliver couldn't breathe. She was wearing the same thing she'd worn to the detachment, except wrapped around her neck was Alex's long red scarf.

TWENTY-FOUR

OLIVER DIDN'T REMEMBER Jameson taking him by the arm and walking him back to the cruiser. He stumbled against it when the ground rose to meet his knees, and his stomach threatened to erupt in dry heaves.

"Stay here," Jameson said. "I don't want you coming back to the site. When the coroner arrives, point her in the right direction, but stay here. All right?"

That wasn't going to be a problem. Oliver couldn't lift his head. He waved a limp hand in Jameson's general direction. "Poor Georgia. She didn't deserve this. She had to be alive and injured when he had her in the barn. That means... Jameson, we have to find this bastard."

"We will. I'm hoping his scent is still on that horse blanket."

Oliver heaved and wiped his mouth. "Or Sid's. What if he's buried her here somewhere?"

Jameson patted his back. "You aren't seeing her right now, are you?"

Of course, Jameson would go there.

"No." He quoted himself. "I have a reasonable expectation of seeing her again. A reasonable expectation..." He raised his head to see Cheswick returning from the crime scene. "Oscar isn't following any other scent here."

Oliver couldn't keep the desperation out of his voice. "Jameson, you have her purse and her phone. Bring them out here before Cheswick leaves with Oscar." The dog looked at his handler as if he understood.

Jameson squinted at Oliver and nodded. "Constable, stick around for a while. I'm bringing in some evidence for Oscar to check out."

"Yes, Sergeant. I'll just get him some food and water. Come on, Oscar. They have another job for you."

A half hour later, the coroner's van arrived. Cheswick waved her over. "You can probably drive across that field. It's pretty solid—hasn't been worked in years."

"Thanks, I'll walk it first." She turned to Oliver. "Who are you, and why are you here?"

Oliver explained as succinctly as he could.

"I see. I'll want to get a full statement from you. Will you carry one of these?"

Oliver held his hands up. "Sorry, Sergeant Jameson doesn't want me at the site."

The coroner rolled her eyes at Cheswick, who held his hands up as well. "Sorry, I'm waiting for evidence for Oscar."

Mumbling to herself, she trudged out the back way through the field, leaving Oliver counting the seconds until Sid's purse arrived.

Cheswick put two bowls on the ground for Oscar and walked back to lean on the cruiser beside Oliver. "What is it we're waiting for?"

"My girlfriend's purse. Sidney Wheeler." Oliver jerked his head toward the woods. "The guy that did this kidnapped Sid."

"Aw. I'm sorry." The two men leaned in silence, watching Oscar eat. After a few moments, Cheswick said, "Oscar is good. I hope he doesn't find her."

"Thanks," was all Oliver could manage.

Thirty minutes later, Sid's purse arrived. Oliver caught sight of it in the evidence bag as the officer rushed past. It was all he could do not to follow him. Watching them all disappear into the woods tore at his heart. *Oscar, please, please, please fail.*

The collection of police vehicles in the yard had attracted attention. An elderly couple walking their dog let him do his business at the end of the road before stopping to talk.

"What's happening? They must have found a body if the coroner's here."

"You might be right." Oliver didn't want to confirm or deny the man's suspicions.

The wife turned to her husband. "I'll bet it has something to do with that Thomas boy, Cole. Remember? He was on the news—kidnapped some poor woman."

Oliver gulped air as if he'd been punched in the stomach, and his reaction didn't go unnoticed. "Now, Betty, don't you be jumping to conclusions."

But Betty could not be stopped. She leaned toward Oliver. "I never trusted that boy. After his mother and Boisvert died in the fire, he went from bad to worse. I still say that if he had come straight to our place on his bike that night, they may not have died."

This was important. Oliver stared at the overgrown foundation that would never give up its secrets. And here was a neighbor who could shed some light on Cole's role that fateful night.

The husband pulled their dog away from Oscar's food. "Don't eat that, Skipper. Well, I hope they catch that little beggar. Let's go, Betty."

Oliver grabbed a notepad from his backpack. "Wait a minute, please. I'm sure the officer in charge here would like to talk to you."

"What for? It was—what? Fifteen years ago?"

Oliver shook his head, his pen poised above the page. "No. Twelve. Nonetheless, I'm sure he'd like to hear what you know about the night of the fire, and especially what you said about Cole."

"I guess." The man fished out his wallet and handed Oliver his card. "He can reach me at that number. We're that first house you come to on the right."

Oliver's hand trembled as he tucked the card in his shirt pocket. "Thanks. I'm sure Sergeant Jameson will be in touch."

* * *

OLIVER HAD ALMOST FORGOTTEN about his stomach when Jameson, the coroner, Cheswick, and Oscar exited the woods. Jameson hollered across the field.

His words thundered in Oliver's ears. "Oscar says she's not here. Oliver, she's not here."

A shudder went through him, bringing him to his knees just as Jameson reached him.

"Oscar found nothing. She was never here. Come on, we'll take you home."

When Jameson and Burns got him upright, Oliver willed his feet to move. *She's not here.* Collapsing on the back seat of the cruiser, he could hear the coroner say, "I'll drive the van over. Can the two of you give me a hand?"

Jameson said, "Of course."

Corporal Cheswick opened Oscar's door for him and picked up his food and water dishes. "We're off, Sergeant. See you back at the detachment."

The officer who'd brought Sid's purse backed his cruiser out after him.

Sid's purse. "Jameson? Jameson!"

The sergeant bent to lean in the window. "Yes, Oliver?"

"Can I have Sid's purse?"

"No, not yet. Here." Jameson handed him a bottle of water through the window.

"Thanks."

"Listen, we won't be long with the coroner, and then I'll get you home."

"Okay." Oliver had to get it together. This wasn't the end of the search; it was just the beginning. By the time the coroner's van drove by and Jameson and Burns returned, Oliver had calmed himself by taking deep breaths and focusing on a little red flashing light on the cruiser's digital display.

Jameson climbed in. "How are you doing back there?"

"Better. Listen, while you were out there with Oscar, a couple came by walking their dog. Dogs are a great excuse for being nosy, but they said some things I think you'll find very interesting."

"About what?"

"About Cole's actions on the night of the fire that killed his mother and his stepfather." Oliver handed the man's card to Jameson. "They live in the first house on the right up ahead."

* * *

IN FRONT of his apartment block, Jameson took Oliver's bike out of the trunk. "Get some sleep tonight. This has been a brutal day for you. I'll follow up with that neighbor this afternoon. By the way, excellent investigative instincts, kid."

"Thanks. I was expecting another rap on the knuckles."

Jameson almost grinned. "I should have anticipated what a bloodhound of a journalist you'd be."

Oliver saw the glance between the two officers as he wheeled his bike through the front door. "Does that mean you'll take me with you tomorrow? After all, I've done all the groundwork up there."

Jameson paused before climbing into the driver's seat. "I'll think about it. If I don't take you, you'll get there on your own anyway, won't you?"

Oliver grinned. "Probably. Besides, I can introduce you to Beatrice so she doesn't sic the dogs on you."

That evening, Oliver expected to see something on the news about the discovery of Georgia's body, but there was nothing new; it wasn't mentioned. Cole Thomas was still dangerous and at large. Sidney Wheeler was still missing and presumed held by Thomas. Anyone having any information…

Oliver willed himself not to imagine the worst. He spent what was left of the day making notes and went to bed wondering if he had to borrow his mother's car again.

When Jameson rang at six the following morning, Oliver was surprised to have slept right through the night. He put it down to his whipsawed emotions the day before.

Forty-five minutes later, he was down on the street as Jameson's cruiser pulled up.

Oliver threw his backpack in the back seat and opened the passenger door in front.

"Sorry, Oliver. No civilians in the front seat."

"That's all right. I don't mind being chauffeured," Oliver said, settling in the back seat. "How did it go with that couple yesterday?"

"You mean Betty and Lionel Withers? Well, Betty makes a mean espresso. She told me the same thing she told you. But Lionel Withers had a bit more to say about the family dynamic. Boisvert moved in with Germaine Thomas shortly after Cole's father died. They never married; she just used his name. Cole had many clashes with Boisvert and frequently ran away from home. They also mentioned him spending the summers on his uncle's fishing boat. They both thought the fire was very suspicious."

Oliver nodded with satisfaction. "What about the investigation?"

Jameson cocked his head to the side. "According to the report, the house was consumed entirely. Well, you saw the foundation. The coroner's report said they must have succumbed to smoke inhalation without waking up. She didn't order autopsies."

"We know they interviewed Cole—you have his fingerprints. Right? What was his story?"

"He claimed Boisvert kicked him out for drinking, so he passed out in the hayloft and didn't hear a thing until the fire trucks arrived. By then, the house was beyond saving." Jameson looked at Oliver in the rearview mirror. "That's plausible, considering how far we had to walk yesterday. And the fire marshal's report corroborates Cole's story."

"He could have set the fire and then gone out to the barn."

"True, but no proof, so the case was closed. The Withers said they had the same thought because of the 'animosity,' as they called it, between Boisvert and Cole. They didn't feel they could come forward with their suspicions because it was 'just an uneasy feeling.'"

Oliver pointed at a Tim Hortons. "Let's get some coffee."

"You sure you want to go through the drive-through like this?"

"No problem. We'll give them something to talk about when I hand them my credit card."

Jameson chuckled. "All right."

For the rest of the trip, they discussed the details of Oliver's previous two trips to Campbell River, especially his conversations with the crabman and Beatrice Flores.

Oliver drank the last drop of his coffee. "You know, I think Beatrice believes Cole murdered her sister and Boisvert, and set the fire to cover it up."

TWENTY-FIVE

"FISHER'S WHARF—THE marina entrance is just there." Oliver pointed.

Jameson parked and donned his cap as they exited the vehicle. "Look, Oliver, you're here as a guide only. At all times, if I tell you to do something, you must comply without hesitation. Do you understand?"

Oliver returned his solid eye contact. "I do."

"All right, then. Which finger is it on?" Jameson shielded his eyes from the glare off the water.

"D, at the far end." The two men walked past the first three fingers from the main dock to D. It seemed every boat was in. Rounding the bow of the *Misty Isle*, Oliver spotted the crab vendor on the dock beside his boat, the *Crabby Joe*. Oliver waved.

"Hello, my name is Oliver Frampton. I bought some crabs off you the other day." Oliver held out his hand.

The crab vendor did the same. "Joe Coville. Yes, I remember you." He held out his hand to Jameson. "Officer."

After the introductions, Oliver asked Joe to repeat what he knew about Cole's appearance at the marina. The times tied in with the red-light image of his truck. His first appearance was early—the morning after Sid's abduction.

"I see the *Clementine* is in. You should talk to Marcus. See if he took Cole out." He nodded in the general direction of slip number thirty-nine.

Jameson thanked him, but not before getting contact information.

Oliver followed Jameson to slip thirty-nine and the *Clementine*. He rapped on the hull. "Mr. Flores?" No answer. A little louder. "Mr. Flores?"

A tousled head of black hair emerged from below. "Yes?"

"Permission to come aboard?" Jameson asked.

"Of course, Officer. But I was just leaving for home. What can I do for you?"

"Mr. Coville tells me your nephew, Cole Thomas, came here twice, looking for you. Did you see him?"

"I saw him early Wednesday morning. I was just about to cast off. He wanted me to take him to one of the logging camps. I said no, of course."

"Did he have anyone with him? A woman, maybe?"

Flores looked confused. "A woman? No."

Jameson tried to keep Oliver from speaking, but Oliver ignored the gesture. "You're sure he didn't have a woman with him, Mr. Flores?"

"No, he didn't." He looked at Jameson. "He was getting belligerent, so I cast off. Left him simmering on the dock."

Oliver interrupted again. "I visited your wife on Wednesday, but she hadn't seen him either."

Marcus Flores looked worried. "Wednesday, you say?"

"Yes."

"I've been trying to reach Bea on the radio since Wednesday, but she doesn't answer. She would have had the radio repaired and not left it out of service like this. That's why I came in early. I'm worried."

Jameson closed his notebook and gave Oliver a stern look. "I'd like to accompany you home, Mr. Flores."

* * *

IN THE PARKING LOT, Jameson informed Flores that Cole could be at the house.

Flores insisted his wife would never let him stay. "He's not welcome in our home."

"Nonetheless, Mr. Flores. Cole is desperate and has resorted to violence and abduction. I don't think you can predict what he will do."

Mr. Flores turned to get into his truck. "I must get home to my wife."

Oliver wasn't sure about Jameson's logic. "When I was there on Wednesday, he was not there. After an initial misunderstanding, your wife accepted a sack of crab I had purchased from Mr. Coville." He pointed back toward the *Crabby Joe*.

"You gave my wife crab?" Flores became even more agitated.

"Yes."

"She would never have accepted them. She is deathly allergic to crab. What did she say?"

"She said, 'I'll have my niece clean them.'"

Panic gripped the man. He jumped into his truck and revved the engine. "I've got to go. We don't have a niece."

Before Mr. Flores could close the door, Jameson held it open, his voice raised over the engine noise. "You must follow me, Mr. Flores. I don't want him to have another hostage."

* * *

FROM THE BACK seat of the cruiser, Oliver looked over his shoulder at Flores, who was hunched over the steering wheel of his truck, the whites of his eyes like golf balls. "We'd better get going before he rear-ends us."

Jameson tapped his radio. "Campbell River, it looks like we may have a hostage situation out there. We're leaving the marina right now. Flores is behind me."

"Copy that. We'll meet you at the highway intersection."

Oliver nodded. "You had them on standby all along?"

Jameson pulled out of the lot with lights and siren. He glanced in the rearview mirror. Flores was on his bumper. "Just as a precaution. Besides, they know the terrain much better than I do."

"You forget that I've been there."

"That means squat compared to the local detachment. Now, at the scene, you are *not* to leave the squad car. Understood?"

"Right."

"I mean it, Frampton. No matter what happens."

Oliver crossed his arms. "I get it. Stay put."

"All right, then."

They arrived at the highway intersection, where the Campbell River cruisers joined them. Oliver checked on Flores. "He's really anxious. You'll probably have more trouble holding him back when we get there."

"This isn't my first rodeo, Oliver."

As they pulled off the highway, Oliver said, "It's about two klicks ahead."

Jameson killed his lights and siren, as did the others. When the corner of the house became visible through the trees, he stopped. He and the other officers assembled beside Flores's truck. Oliver could see them having a logistical discussion, pointing and consulting with the anxious Marcus. Jameson opened the driver's door and escorted him right back to the cruiser. He opened Oliver's door, and Flores got in.

"Stay with Oliver, Mr. Flores. We don't want either of you getting in the way."

Marcus stuck his foot in the door before Jameson could close it. "You're not locking me in, Sergeant."

Jameson looked back at the other officers, who were already dispersing. He shook his head. "All right, Mr. Flores. But don't, under any circumstances, interfere with this operation. We don't want you accidentally shot. Do you understand me?" Jameson glared around Flores at Oliver. "Frampton, you know what we're dealing with here."

He turned to join the advancing officers, leaving the door ajar. They approached the house, using outbuildings, vehicles, and a boat for cover. When they were within forty meters of the front door, Jameson hailed Cole on a loudspeaker.

Flores pushed the door open. "I know a back way in."

Oliver grabbed him by the arm and pulled him back. "You're not going anywhere. You want to get shot?"

Flores was difficult to dissuade. His distress filled the air with the scent of salt water, fresh fish, and sweat. As the minutes ticked by, Flores became more and more agitated, until he tore free of Oliver's grip and plunged into the road. Oliver scrambled across the seat and out the door after him. Flores was already at the edge of the bush. Chasing him down would be no small feat, but Oliver leaped over fallen logs like a hurdler and tackled him to the ground.

The back of the house was within view, but Oliver could not see Jameson or the others from this angle. Then, just at that moment, the back door swung open, and Cole bailed out with a backpack and headed for the trees about twenty meters ahead of them.

Oliver covered Flores's mouth with one hand and pulled out his phone with the other. He hit Jameson's number with his thumb.

"Jameson, I'm in the trees at the back of the house with Flores. Cole has just run into the woods ahead of us. I don't think he's armed. Come around the west side of the house, and I'll stand up and point you in the right direction."

Within seconds, Oliver and Flores were out in the open, waving and pointing Jameson and the other officers toward the spot where Cole had entered the woods. Oliver nodded vigorously. "Yes!" The officers spread out and charged into the woods.

His head spun to the back door. Flores had already scaled the steps.

TWENTY-SIX

TORMENTED howls reached Oliver's ears before he got through the door. He burst into the kitchen to find Flores on his knees, cradling his wife's head in his arms and moaning, "Bea. Bea."

Oliver kneeled beside him and felt her neck for a pulse. "She's alive, Marcus. Call 9-1-1. I have to find Sid."

Flores didn't respond. Oliver shook his shoulder. "Marcus. Call for an ambulance. Now!" Flores laid his wife's head gently on the floor and reached for his phone.

Oliver sprang to his feet, every muscle in his body taut. He dodged from room to room. "Sid! Sid!" He could hear a faint thumping. "Sid?" There it was again. He threw open every door downstairs, but nothing.

Rapid thumps—louder now. He glanced up the stairs and bounded up two at a time. "Sid!" He opened one, two, then three bedroom doors. The thumping grew louder still, along with a muffled cry.

"Sid. The en suite."

Oliver gagged. It wasn't just the unflushed toilet or the flies on the uneaten food on the floor. It was Sid, jammed between the bathtub and the toilet, tears streaming down her cheeks. Raw flesh oozed around her taped mouth. Her wrists bled from the rope lashing her hands to her ankles. Oliver could not even get his arms around her with her knees bent up to her chin. Her eyes and muffled screams begged him to take the tape from her mouth.

Oliver picked at the edges, a reluctant growl emanating from his throat. "It's tearing your skin."

Sid shook her head so violently she yanked the tape from his grip and freed her lips. "Tear it off! Tear it off!"

Her screams tore his heart out. When she bit the rope at her wrists, Oliver took the rope from her mouth and untied her hands. Freed, she threw her arms around Oliver's neck. He lifted her out and held her until her sobs subsided. "He's gone, Sid. He's gone."

Oliver touched her temple with the whisper of a kiss and lowered her onto the edge of the tub. "Let me get your feet free." The knots were so tight he needed his pocketknife. All the while, Sid clung to his shirt and buried her face in his neck. Once he had severed the rope, the chain that had kept her prisoner fell from the intake pipe.

He lifted her into his arms and sat on the edge of the bathtub. He kissed her eyes—the only part of her face he felt it was safe to kiss. "What has he done to you?"

She wrapped her arms around his neck and shook her head. "Just get me out of here. Where's Bea? Is she okay?"

"Downstairs. Can you walk?"

"Yes! I could run." Sid's face puckered with sobs. Oliver guided her out the door and down the stairs. She balked at the doorway to the kitchen. "Is he gone? Is he really gone?"

"Yes. He ran into the bush with five officers on his tail."

When she saw Mr. Flores holding his wife's head, she fell to the floor beside her. "Oh, no. Beatrice." She took her hand and held it.

In the distance, a siren wailed, and Beatrice opened her eyes.

* * *

OLIVER LEFT SID sitting on the floor beside Beatrice and met the paramedics at the front door. He waved them in.

The first paramedic asked for the patient's name and instructed Marcus and Sid to move away from her.

"Can you tell me what happened here?"

Marcus circled his finger in the air. "They were held hostage by my crazy nephew, Cole Thomas. My wife has a gash on her head."

To Oliver, the paramedic said, "Where is this nephew now?"

"The police are chasing him down as we speak." Oliver waved his hand toward the bush. He knew they had to establish a safe environment before treating their patient.

Satisfied there was no danger, the paramedic began his preliminary examination. "Are you Mr. Flores?"

"Yes."

"Do you know how long she has been unconscious?"

Marcus looked at Oliver for help.

"Marcus and I got into the house about twenty minutes ago. He called 9-1-1 immediately. Marcus, did she come around at all while I was upstairs?"

"She moaned a bit, but she never opened her eyes until we heard your siren."

"That's good. Mrs. Flores? Beatrice? My name is Rick. I'm a paramedic. Can you hear me?"

Bea opened her eyes and mumbled, "Yes. Oh, my head."

"Yes, you've got quite the gash there. We're going to take you to the hospital and get that fixed up for you. All right?"

Beatrice blinked and reached for Marcus.

Rick said, "Mr. Flores, would you come and hold her hand while we get the stretcher in here?"

As soon as Marcus mentioned Sid was also a hostage, the second paramedic, Gordon, focused on her. He examined her face, wrists, and ankles, as well as multiple contusions on her arms, legs, and ribs.

When he lifted her left elbow, she winced. "Did you fall on this?"

"Yes, it's quite painful."

"You seem to have restricted range of motion. It could be a bone bruise or chipped, so best to have that x-rayed. Excuse me." Gordon joined Rick, who was wheeling in the stretcher.

Once they had lifted Bea onto the stretcher, guided it outside, and lifted her into the ambulance, Rick turned to Oliver. "Mr. Flores will come with us. Can you follow us to the hospital?"

"I don't have a vehicle here, but... Marcus, could I take your truck?"

Nodding, Marcus threw him the keys and climbed into the ambulance beside his wife.

It was a longer walk to the truck than Oliver anticipated, but Sid wouldn't let him leave her to bring it closer. She balked at getting in at first, but with gentle encouragement, Oliver managed to lift her in.

"Open the windows—all the way. Olly. I need them open—all of them."

Oliver held her hand as he drove. Her mental state was more of a concern at that moment than her physical condition. When the ambulance reached the highway, their lights and siren startled her. "It's okay, Sid. You're safe." He kissed her hand. The ambulance escorted them straight to the emergency entrance. Oliver parked and walked Sid in right behind Bea's stretcher.

When Sid saw Bea's hand reach for Marcus, she said, "I'm right behind you, Bea." They watched her disappear behind a wall of white coats.

"Let's get you admitted, Sid." Oliver guided her to the admissions window, answered all their questions, and even produced her health care number from his phone.

Sid still clung to his arm. "My purse?"

Oliver smiled down at her. "No. The police still have it. I got it off your prescription."

The clerk directed them to the waiting room. "A nurse will be with you shortly." The PA system barked out doctors' names and orders with calm urgency.

Oliver hoped it wouldn't be long—Sid still trembled in his arms. Just as she sagged, a nurse appeared.

"She's in shock. I'll get a stretcher."

"No need." Oliver scooped her into his arms and pushed past the nurse and through the swinging doors.

When Oliver laid her on the bed in the cubicle, Sid opened her eyes and clung to him. The nurse was very attentive. She smiled and tucked a warm blanket around her. Then she gently wrapped a blood-pressure cuff on Sid's bruised arm. Sid rested her injured arm across her chest while the nurse took her vitals.

"Your blood pressure is fine, Sidney. I'll get you some water, and we'll have a look at your injuries. Here's a gown. Young man, you can go back to the waiting room."

"No. He's staying." Sid wouldn't let go of his arm.

Thank goodness. Oliver wasn't about to leave her side. "She's been traumatized and needs me here."

"That's fine. I'll give you a few minutes to get undressed and bring you another nice, warm blanket, okay?"

It was all Oliver could do not to gasp at the sight of Sid's bruises and raw skin. Although he wanted to kiss her, he could not. The skin around her mouth glistened with blood.

That nurse had it timed to the second. She appeared with warm blankets the moment he laid Sid's head on the pillow. She tucked them around Sid's body up to her neck and wrapped her feet. "Dr. Thurlow will be in to see you shortly, Sidney. Are you comfortable?"

"Yes, I'm okay, as long as Olly's here." She pulled his hand under the blanket.

Oliver placed a chair alongside Sid's bed and never took his eyes off her face. As the minutes ticked by, she became calmer. He could even feel her grip on his hand relax. It wasn't long before the curtains parted and two women in white coats entered, smiling at Sid.

"Hello, Sidney. My name is Dr. Thurlow, and this is Nurse Belmont. She is a psychologist."

"Hello, Sidney. Call me Charlie. And who's this young man?"

"I'm Oliver Frampton, Sid's lesser half."

"Oh, you're married?"

Oliver smiled at Sid and teared up. "Not yet."

Dr. Thurlow examined Sid's face, wrists, and ankles. "We'll get these cleaned up and some soothing ointment applied right away, Sidney. Let's have a look at your other abrasions and contusions." She pulled back the blanket just enough.

Sidney winced when she touched her elbow and ribs.

"Well, Sidney, I think we should get a few x-rays." She called in a nurse to dress Sid's ankles and wrists and apply an ointment to her face. No sooner was that done than an X-ray technician arrived with a wheelchair.

Oliver helped her into the chair and tucked the blanket around her legs. Charlie stooped and took both Sidney's hands in hers.

"Oliver can't go with you for this, Sidney. Are you okay with that?"

The technician smiled. "I promise I don't bite."

This seemed to be enough reassurance for Sid, and she let go of Oliver's hand.

As she turned Sid around, Charlie said, "I'll go with Sidney. Are you going to be all right?"

Oliver nodded, but as soon as the curtain closed, he sat down hard, put his face in his hands, and crashed.

* * *

IN THE HAZE of his tormented thoughts, he tried to regroup. *Get your shit together, Frampton.* He grabbed a handful of tissues and wiped his face. But that couldn't hide his twisted expression and trembling hands. When Charlie opened the curtain again, he knew she could tell.

"Oliver, Sidney's coming back. Could you come with me while they get her settled? I have some paperwork for you." She put her hand on Oliver's shoulder and ushered him out of the cubicle just as the X-ray tech wheeled Sidney in.

"Thanks. I guess I kind of lost it in there. He's held her hostage since last Monday. I didn't know if she was dead or alive. We found the body of one of his victims on Thursday. I've been going crazy." Oliver couldn't stem his verbal diarrhea.

"You're entitled to lose it. You've done a great job of holding it together for Sidney's sake."

"This whole thing was my fault." Oliver sat, rubbing his thighs.

"Funny, Sidney was just saying the same thing. She sees the pain in your face and blames herself."

"No. No way is this her fault." He tried to get up, but she restrained him with a gentle touch on the shoulder.

"You are right, but you both need to acknowledge that this is no one's fault but the man who did this to Sidney. Are you ready to go in there and tell her so?"

Oliver took a deep breath and huffed. He stood and shook his shoulders. "Whether I'm ready or not, I have to be with her."

* * *

WHEN OLIVER PARTED THE CURTAINS, Sid was being tucked in again. She reached for him. He dodged around the nurse and kissed her hand. "I'm afraid to kiss you. I don't want to hurt you."

Sid tried to smile. "Ow. It's just as well. You'd probably slide off my face."

"Have they seen the X-rays yet?"

"The radiologist and Dr. Thurlow are checking them now." Sid took a long look at Oliver's eyes. "You've been crying. I'm so sorry, Olly. I should never have walked over to his truck. This is all my fault."

Oliver shook his head and almost put his finger on her lips. "No way. If I hadn't opened Alex's case, none of this would have happened. Cole wouldn't have…" He stopped just short of saying Georgia's name.

"You're not responsible for Cole's actions. And besides, if you hadn't opened Alex's case, we never would have discovered what happened to her. Would you want that on your conscience?"

Oliver rolled his eyes, rocked his head from side to side, and grunted. "No, but we still haven't found her." He tried not to make eye contact with Alex, sitting on the other side of Sid's bed. It was the first time she had appeared since Georgia's interview.

Sid squeezed his hand. "Olly, I'll give up my guilt only if you give up yours."

"Okay, on the count of three: one, two, three." They both made little explosion sounds with hand gestures.

Dr. Thurlow came through the curtains. "What's this?"

Sid tried to smile. "Just killing some ghosts."

"Sounds good. Now, about your X-rays. No broken ribs, but there is a small chip on your elbow."

Oliver asked, "What is the treatment for that?"

"The good news is it won't require surgery. The bad news is it will require splinting for several weeks while it heals on its own. You'll ice it for the swelling, and I'll give you an anti-inflammatory and an analgesic for the pain."

As she spoke, a nurse arrived to apply Sid's splint.

Oliver squeezed Sid's hand. "I can take her home, then?"

"Yes, you can, but she's had a sedative and a painkiller, so you'll have to support her until you get her to bed."

"I can do that." Then he snickered and held up his hands. "Wait a minute—we don't have a ride back to Nanaimo."

"Not to worry. There's an RCMP sergeant wearing the pattern off the floor tiles in the waiting room."

* * *

AS SOON AS Oliver wheeled Sid through the automatic doors, Jameson was on his feet, his eyes darting between them. "Oliver?"

"She's going to be okay. A bone chip on her elbow." He kissed her on the top of the head. "Sid, you remember Sergeant Jameson?"

Jameson took off his cap. "Hello again, Sidney. Let's get you in the car and on the road home."

Jameson had his cruiser parked right in front of the door. Once Oliver had Sid settled in the back seat, he tucked a blanket around her. "Sorry, not fresh out of the oven like in the ER."

"That's okay. I've got your arms to keep me warm."

With Sid snuggled against his chest, Oliver glanced at Jameson in the rearview mirror and grinned. "I will never have another opportunity to repeat this slightly modified quote to an actual Mountie: Home, Jameson, and don't spare the horses."

TWENTY-SEVEN

OLIVER SIGHED when Sid fell asleep. "I'm glad they gave her a sedative. I hope she sleeps the rest of the way."

Jameson's voice was barely audible. "How is she really, Oliver? It looks like he taped her face. Tell me what happened at the house."

Blinking back his tears, Oliver stroked her arm and kissed her forehead. "Jameson, if Cole had been in that house, I swear you'd be arresting me for murder."

It took a minute for him to swallow the frog in his throat before he could recount the horrific state he had found her in, the situation with Bea, and their drive behind the ambulance in Flores's truck. "I tell you, Jameson, there was a psych nurse in the ER who talked me off the ledge. I lost it when they took Sid to X-ray. She looked so broken and vulnerable. It's going to take a while before either of us gets over this."

"Absolutely." Jameson drove on in silence for an hour before speaking. "Oliver, you're lucky to have Sid."

"Thanks. I know. Do you have someone, Jameson?"

Jameson grinned from ear to ear. "We have Thomas."

Oliver almost jarred Sid awake. "What? No shit?"

"No shit. I got the call when I was in the waiting room."

"How? Where?"

"First, I want to know how you and Flores just happened to be behind the house when I explicitly told you two to stay put."

"I tried, but I couldn't hold Flores back, so I gave chase. I tackled him at the edge of the bush just as Cole ran out the back door. I was afraid he was going to attract Cole's attention, so I covered his mouth and called you."

"Well, it's a good thing you consistently disobey orders, because he would have been long gone if you hadn't. The five of us spread out and chased him through those woods. When we came out on another road, Cole was almost out of sight. He must have had his truck hidden on that road all the time.

"The Campbell River officers radioed his position while we trekked back to our vehicles. By the time we got there, the ambulance had left and Flores's truck was gone. By the way, I inquired about the condition of Mrs. Flores, and they said they'd be keeping her in for a few days for observation. Did you think to leave his truck keys?"

Oliver patted his pockets. "Yes. When I registered Sid, I left them for Marcus." He wound up the air on his finger. "Back to the story."

"Right. On the highway, a CR unit spotted Thomas's truck heading for the marina, so they gave chase. Unfortunately, Cole bailed from his truck crossways of the gangway, which gave him enough time to cast off the *Clementine*."

"He stole his uncle's boat?"

"Yup. And by the time the RCMP boat was summoned, he was long gone."

Oliver rolled his eyes. "So you have him 'cornered'—someplace in the Salish Sea?"

Jameson nodded his head like a bobble head. "Just wait. I have to let the drama build. We've been waiting a long time for this moment. Let's savor it."

Oliver smirked. "All right, all right."

Jameson pulled up to the curb in front of the apartment. "What

Cole didn't realize was that he couldn't turn off the GPS without disabling his navigation system. Plus, the RCMP boat had—wait for it..." Jameson poked his finger in the air as he opened Oliver's door. "A lot more 'horsepower.'"

* * *

OLIVER GAVE his keys to Jameson before he lifted Sid from the back seat. He took a deep breath of the cool evening air. "That is the easiest breath I've taken in a week."

Jameson walked in front of him and held the door. "I can believe it."

Oliver turned sideways to carry Sid past his bike in the hall. "Thanks, Jameson. I guess we'll be seeing you shortly?"

"Of course. I'll call you when I have Cole in custody, and we'll see if Sid is feeling up to an interview."

"Right. And thanks for the lift, Jameson."

"No problem. Good night."

Oliver carried Sid into the bedroom and laid her on the bed. He took off her shoes, and he was about to cover her up when she spoke, her words interrupted by groggy sighs.

"Olly, I need... a shower... Help me?"

"But your splint and bandages..."

"Take them off... please? I can't stand... these clothes."

"All right." He carried her into the bathroom and sat her on the shower bench. "You won't fall?"

"No. I'm okay." She sat with her head hanging while Oliver undressed.

"Now it's your turn." He undid the Velcro straps holding the splint in place, removed the bandages from her wrists, and helped her out of her clothes. His jaw clenched at the sight of her bruises and scrapes. "Can you stand? Put your arm around my neck."

Oliver held her in the warm stream and washed her hair. The shampoo streamed down her face. "Does that sting?"

"Yes. But it feels... wonderful."

She murmured as Oliver rinsed her hair and soaped her body. He thought of the days he had spent terrified he'd lost her. In this tender moment, he realized how much he loved her. He rinsed her body with gentle strokes over abrasions and blackened ribs.

"Sit down while I dry you off. I don't want to touch your face with the towel. Can you dry your hair?"

"Just put the towel on the pillow. I need to… lie down."

She was fading fast. Oliver helped her to the bed, spread her wet curls on the towel, patted her delicate body dry, and pulled the duvet up to her chin.

"I'll get the bandages and the ice pack for your elbow."

She smiled and closed her eyes. "Mm-hm."

When he returned, she was fast asleep. Her eyelashes didn't even flutter when he lifted her arm out from under the duvet and set the ice pack on her swollen elbow. He left the ice pack in place while he dressed her wrists and ankles.

Wincing, he cradled her arm to reapply the splint and glanced at her face as he tucked her arms back under the duvet. The raw skin on her face still glistened with ointment. He sat beside her, watching her sleep so peacefully, and wept.

* * *

WHEN OLIVER AWOKE, the morning sun streamed through the window onto Sid's smiling face.

"Good morning," she said.

Oliver raised to his elbow. "Good morning to you, too. How do you feel?"

"Not too bad—a bit stiff and sore. The elbow aches, but I took a pill." She touched the corner of her mouth. "Could use a bit more ointment. It's starting to crack." Her eyes grew wide. "And I brushed the fur off my teeth! Thanks for last night. You were wonderful."

"It was like washing my mother's fine crystal. I was afraid I'd drop you and you'd shatter into a thousand pieces."

"Well, I'm not that fragile. Now that the sedative has worn off, I'm not so rubbery."

She rolled away from him. "Spoon with me, Olly. I need to feel your skin against mine."

Oliver slipped his arm under her splint and cupped her breast in his hand. When he kissed her neck, she pressed her bottom against him.

"I love you, Sidney Wheeler."

* * *

TWO DAYS PASSED before Jameson called to say that the Campbell River detachment had transferred Cole Thomas down to Nanaimo. "How is Sid?"

"Not too shabby." Oliver wrapped an arm around her waist and kissed her forehead. He was hesitant to kiss her lips, with her cheeks and mouth still looking red and angry. "What's the plan?"

"I want to interview Sid. Is she feeling up to it today?"

Oliver looked to Sid for the nod. "She says sure, but you still have her wheels. You'll have to pick us up."

"We should be able to release it today. I'll pick you up at ten o'clock?"

"We'll be ready." He searched Sid's eyes. "How do you feel about seeing Cole again?"

"I'm not afraid of him now—just pissed off. I mean, we've known him since he was eighteen. He was a bully and a punk then, and he still is. It's as if he's stuck in a time warp."

"I can relate to the time warp analogy." Oliver hadn't thought of Alex since the hospital, and even then, she had been quiet. She must have guessed he didn't need any help beating himself up. He took Sid's bandaged wrists in his hands and gently stroked them with his thumbs. "You haven't told me what happened. Are you trying to spare me?"

Sid gave a sideways glance at the omelet cooling on her plate. "Of course not, but I know you're going to overreact when Jameson wheedles every last detail out of me. Come on. Let's eat before he gets here."

He sat, resting his forearms on the table. "It's just that I look at what he's done to you, and I... I imagine..."

She reached over and squeezed his hand. "Don't. Don't imagine that kind of abuse. What you see is all of it."

They ate in silence, although he couldn't stop seeing her in the state he'd found her. He pushed his plate away, his omelet half-finished.

Promptly at ten, Jameson rang the doorbell. When he saw Sid, he smiled. "You look great. How do you feel?"

"Liar. But I feel a lot better than the last time you saw me."

Oliver led her to the curb by the hand, his need to protect her unabated even while being escorted by an armed Mountie.

A couple passing on the sidewalk gave them a second glance as they climbed into the back seat of the cruiser. Oliver snickered. "The neighbors are getting suspicious with police cars at our door so often."

"I could use the lights and siren? Maybe put you in handcuffs."

"I'll pass. You want us to get evicted?"

At the detachment, Jameson put on his game face. He opened the door to an interview room and ushered them in. "Have a seat, and I'll get the files."

Oliver moved his chair closer to Sid and put his arm around her shoulders. The thought of Cole being nearby made his entire body tense.

Sid wiped his sweaty brow. "Olly, you don't look so good."

"Well, I'm not." He pulled at the neck of his T-shirt. His throat was dry.

Jameson strode in. "You all right?"

Oliver slammed his fist on his thigh. "He's in this building, isn't he?"

"Yes. You're going to be in the same building with him a few times, Oliver, when this comes to trial, so you'd better rein in that anger. And if Sid wants you here, you are going to keep quiet. Right?"

"Right. But when I think of what he's done to Sid, I…"

Sid rubbed his knee. "Come on. I'm fine now. Let's get on with this."

"Right you are, Sid." Jameson's eyes darted between them as he opened a file labeled *Sidney Wheeler*. "Could you start with the Monday night while you were working at the university bookstore?"

"I told Olly I was going to the pub after work with Miriam and some friends. I don't need my phone at work, so I didn't notice it wasn't in my purse. You do have it, don't you?"

Jameson nodded. "Yes, it's in evidence. Go on."

"When I got to the parking lot, Cole was leaning against my car. I told the girls to go on without me, and that I hadn't seen Cole since graduation day. Since you were looking for him, I wanted them to have his name."

"If you were already suspicious of Cole, why didn't you just go with the girls?"

"It was something he said: 'I know who killed Alex, and I have proof.' I wanted to see what he had."

"I'm going to show you the security video from VIU of that exchange."

As the video played, Sid squeezed the blood out of Oliver's hand.

"Right there. He's telling me he has the evidence in his truck."

Jameson interrupted her at the point where Sid tried to turn back.

"Why did you turn back there?"

"I wanted my phone, but he said it would only take a minute."

Oliver started to squirm. He wanted to be angry with her for trusting Cole, even for a minute, but Jameson gave him a look that said *don't go there*.

Jameson paused the surveillance video. "You walked out of video range. What happened at his truck?"

"I don't think he initially had any intention of kidnapping me. He opened the passenger door and took the scarf out of a paper bag. He said it was Alex's, and that Georgia had strangled her with it. I recognized it right away. I knew it was hers. She wore it almost every day."

Oliver got up and sat down again. Alex sat in the corner, twirling that very same scarf. *All these years, and the clues were right in front of me. I'm so sorry, Alex.* He swallowed hard; he had almost said that out loud.

Jameson handed him a bottle of water and urged Sid to continue.

"I asked him why he didn't turn it over to the police, and he said it was because he knew Georgia had set him up. He wanted me to make sure Oliver had seen Georgia follow Alex into the park.

"I made the mistake of asking him how he knew Oliver had been in the park the night Alex disappeared. He got this confused look on his face, and then he looked genuinely frightened. I turned to run back to my car. That's when he hit me from behind."

"Were you unconscious?"

"I fell, and that's when I hurt my elbow. Before I knew it, he was straddling the back of my legs and tying my hands together behind my back. I struggled, but it was futile. My elbow hurt like hell. He tied my feet together while I was still on my stomach on the asphalt. I still wonder why he had that rope handy. Maybe it *was* premeditated."

She paused, looking at the ceiling for a moment.

"He kept saying over and over that he didn't want to do this, but that now he needed something to negotiate with because Georgia had set him up."

Jameson gave Oliver an "I told you so" glance as Sid spoke.

"He hoisted me into the back seat of his truck and drove out of that lot like a maniac. When he opened the glove compartment, I saw a handgun, and I must have gasped. He didn't verbally threaten me with it; he just looked at me to make sure I saw it."

Jameson turned off the surveillance video. "We know that he

immediately headed northwest to Campbell River and went to the marina the next morning. Where were you?"

"Lying or sitting in the back seat the whole time. It was hard to keep my balance—the rope was tight. I thought about trying to strangle him or kick him in the head, but with that gun…"

Oliver clenched his fists in his pockets while Sid described her vain effort to escape at the marina. Unable to kick out the window, she tried to reach the horn, but got jammed between the seats. Her obvious reluctance to elaborate on the two miserable nights she spent trussed up in that truck with Cole was making Oliver's frustration worse.

Sid took a long drink of water before continuing. "As soon as the sun was up the next morning, he drove back to the marina. When his uncle's boat pulled away from the dock, I could see Cole waving his arms and giving him the finger. I was terrified when he drove back to the same place on that back road. He left me in the truck and took off through the woods. I tried to get free, but it was hopeless. The rope was digging into my skin. After a while, he came back, untied my feet, and dragged me back into the woods. And he took the gun. I've never been so scared in my life. I was sure he had been digging my grave."

Sid looked down at her feet and squeezed Oliver's hand. He glared at Jameson. *Stop her!*

Jameson caught his drift and turned off the video. "Let's take a break."

* * *

THE CEDAR BENCH in the small green space behind the detachment was the ideal spot to decompress.

"I'll leave you here. Take your time with your coffee. Come back in when you're ready." Jameson left them to unwind in the dappled sunlight.

Oliver put his arm around Sid and pulled her close. The tension in the interview room had followed them out, but as the minutes passed, it dissipated.

Wildflowers sprouted haphazardly around the perimeter, held at bay by occasional mowing. He pointed out a lone tiger lily nodding at the edge of the woods.

Sid smiled and leaned against his chest. "Alone, its regal poise calming conscious thought."

Oliver smiled. "I like that." They finished their coffee in silence.

He drank the last drop and kissed her head. "Ready?"

She nodded. "Let's go for it."

Back in the interview room, Jameson turned on the video recorder. Sid began from when she'd seen the house through the trees. "The relief I felt at that moment almost took me to my knees. I was hoping maybe it was an empty house and he might leave me there and take off, but when he pushed me in the back door, he called out for Beatrice.

"She came downstairs, just livid, yelling about her husband calling from the boat. But she backed up when Cole brandished the gun in her face. He was becoming more and more irrational. He said, 'Marcus will trade the boat for you,' meaning Bea.

"She tried her best to reason with him. She even made lunch and tried to put sleeping pills in his food, but when he told her to give that plate to me, she 'accidentally' dumped it on the floor.

"Cole was the first to hear you coming up the drive. He grabbed Bea and stood behind her at the window. When he recognized you, he grabbed me by the arm and held the gun to my head. He told Bea to get rid of you or else. I could hardly breathe."

Oliver got up and placed his hands on her shoulders. "I was that close to her, Jameson. And I missed the clue about the crab allergy. I mean, she held the bag at arm's length. Dammit."

Sid reached up and squeezed his fingers. "Stop this. That doesn't necessarily follow."

Jameson motioned for Oliver to resume his seat. "Let's get back to the sequence of events."

Sid clutched Oliver's hand to her chest and looked up into his eyes. "Because Bea told you she'd never take him in, Cole relaxed a little when you left, thinking you'd never be back. Then something seemed to suddenly occur to him—something frightening—and he started texting, a lot. He became more and more agitated with each text. That's when he tied me to the pipe in the bathroom upstairs. I heard him leave in Bea's car."

Her tears boiled over, scalding Oliver's heart. He couldn't hold her tight enough.

Jameson left the room. He must have been watching on the monitor, because he didn't return until they had regained their composure, and he came bearing gifts of more coffee and donuts. What else?

After a sip of coffee and a nod of approval, Jameson changed the direction of the interview. "Sid, during those three days, did Cole mention Alex's disappearance?"

"Yes. He was obsessed with trying to justify what he was doing. But his rants were so erratic, I didn't know what I felt half the time: abject fear, anger, or pity. I talked about Alex a lot, about how the three of us were friends back then and how sad it made Olly when she died. I didn't ask questions."

"You said 'friends.' And 'died'?"

"Yes, deliberately. I wanted to see his reaction. That got him preening about what a jock he had been in high school. He said Georgia had sworn him to secrecy so he'd help her move the body. He kept insisting he had nothing to do with her death—that he'd just helped Georgia out of a jam. 'And then she double-crossed me,' he said. He insisted Georgia had strangled Alex—but not when she followed Alex into the park from Connie's."

Oliver was on his feet. "I knew it! That explains the time gap." He paced back and forth in the small room.

Jameson's eyebrows popped up, and Sid said, "What gap?"

"We've always thought Alex was killed shortly after she left Connie's, right? Late afternoon? But she—at least my memory of her—came to me around nine thirty that night, when I was at my lowest point emotionally."

Suddenly, it all made sense. Alex had always said he had a 'cosmic gift' for sensing the moment someone close to him died.

Sid pieced together the essence of Cole's rants. Georgia had met up with Alex at the duck pond, crying about her confrontation with Morgan. After Georgia goaded her like only Georgia could, they got into a shoving match. Alex went over backward and hit her head on a rock. Georgia, sure she was dead, dragged Alex's body into the shrubbery. Knowing Alex could easily be found, she coerced Cole into going back after dark to move the body.

But when they got there, Alex had regained consciousness, although she was disoriented. Cole told Sid that he and Georgia had fought and that he'd left shortly after. Later, Georgia told him that she'd heard someone coming on the path. She'd panicked, and strangled Alex to keep her quiet.

"At that point, Cole realized she had made him an accomplice, so he helped her 'dispose' of the body."

Oliver sank into his chair. "Oh my god. Poor Alex." The utter futility of his search for Alex crushed him. "You know what this means? If Cole had protected Alex that night instead of leaving her with Georgia, none of this would have happened, and it would have been over twelve years ago."

Jameson said, "Don't lose heart, Oliver. At least now we know Cole can lead us to her." He directed the interview back to Sid. "How did Cole act when he returned on Friday?"

"Like he had just settled a score." Sid shook her head. "I didn't want to believe it, but Bea guessed he'd killed Georgia. I thought Bea was reckless to challenge him about it—and to accuse him of setting the fire that killed her sister and Boisvert."

"Yes, that was foolhardy of Bea. It probably explains a lot of her injuries."

Sid continued, "Cole concentrated on monitoring the transmissions from the *Clementine* after that. Marcus was obviously getting concerned because Bea wasn't answering. Cole figured Marcus would return earlier. And he was right—Marcus headed back. Cole was still bent on getting away by boat."

"How did he know we were closing in?"

"He didn't. He knew exactly when the *Clementine* would get in, so he prepared to steal the boat while Marcus was on his way home."

"Coincidentally, he did just that." Jameson turned off the video and slapped the file closed.

TWENTY-EIGHT

THE MOOD WAS glum over breakfast. Sid stirred her eggs. "What's taking so long? It's been two days."

"I don't know. Jameson probably has a casebook strategy—let Cole stew for a while before interviewing him. Body language and all that." Oliver frowned. "You've got to eat something, Sid."

"My stomach is upset. What if they don't get a confession out of him? Isn't my word and Bea's just hearsay?"

"I don't know."

Sid shoved her plate away and dragged her heels over to her easel. Holding the palette with her splinted hand was awkward. It clattered out of her grasp before she could squeeze paint onto it. "Damn. What *do* you know, Olly? What if they can't find her body? He'll get away with it."

Sid wouldn't normally snap at him. "You know as much as I do, Sid. There is a string of charges against him right now. Who knows? He may try to use Alex as leverage." He scraped Sid's breakfast into the garbage.

Squeezing paint directly onto the canvas, Sid began with broad, angular strokes. "What am I doing? This wasn't supposed to be art therapy." She cocked her head to the side and stuck her brush in the cleaner.

She needed to get her mind off all this. Oliver came up behind her and kissed her neck; he felt her relax against him.

"I'm sorry, Olly."

He turned her in his arms and kissed her lips as tenderly as he could. "I get it. I'll give Jameson a call."

The call went to voice mail. "It's Oliver. What's happening with Cole? Has he told you where they took Alex? Call me." He hung up and shrugged. "Jameson will call. He won't leave us hanging."

Sid sat on the sofa with her feet up on the coffee table. "Why don't we drive out there? I want to see where the house was, and..." She swallowed. "And where you found Georgia."

"Why? I'd have thought that's the last place you'd want to be."

"I don't know. It's the way Bea talked about her sister and growing up out there. They had a relatively carefree childhood. Bea had no children, so it was doubly painful to lose her sister and to find only disappointment in Cole."

"All right. We'll go. But we may not get onto the site. It *is* still a crime scene." Oliver lifted her feet gently off the table—her ankles were still weeping. "Get dressed. You want any help... with your splint, I mean?"

"Meh, I could probably manage." But she grinned and took him by the hand into the bedroom.

* * *

THE DRIVE OUT was nowhere near as exhilarating as biking would have been, but Oliver's pulse quickened when the farm entrance came into view. Several cruisers lined the roadway and clogged the farmyard.

Oliver slammed his fist on the dash. "Son of a... They're already here."

Sid drove up right behind a cruiser, blocking the driveway, and parked. "Let's see them get out of there now."

Walking into the farmyard, Oliver lifted the crime scene tape for Sid. "They must be out by the barn or in the woods." They skirted the overgrown foundation. "This is it—totally consumed except for those rusted-out appliances. I'll bet Cole watched it burn."

Sid shook her head in consternation. "According to Bea, he was home that night."

"The neighbors told me the same thing." Oliver pointed down the road.

Sid hugged Oliver's arm. "Do you think he killed them first?"

"Let's hope Jameson can get it out of him. Come on. I'll take you to the barn."

As soon as they had cleared the tree line surrounding the farmyard, they could see a few uniforms at the barn and across the field, very near where they'd entered the woods the day they found Georgia's body.

"Come on." Oliver took Sid's hand. Heading into the field, an officer at the barn hailed them. They turned and walked in her direction.

"You are not allowed here. This is a crime scene."

"I'm fully aware of that, Officer. Call Sergeant Jameson and tell him Oliver Frampton is here."

Without taking her eyes off them, she made the call. When she hung up, she said, "I'm to escort you to the site and keep an eye on you. You tend not to follow orders, it seems."

"Thank you, Officer." Together, they walked through the neglected field and the blackberry thicket. Another officer met them and led them further. Tape wound around tree trunks and shrubs before disappearing into dense bush. They followed it for about fifty meters but saw no activity.

"This is as far as you go." The second officer ducked under the tape and looked at the first officer. "Watch them."

Faint voices drifted between the trees. Oliver put his arm around Sid's shoulders and pulled her to him.

He could hear Cole's voice, as defiant as ever. "It was a long time ago. It's around here someplace. It was dark, and I never came back. Why would I?"

Sid's arms tightened around him.

Several officers were digging in various places between the trees. Jameson came out and approached them. "I was hoping to find her before I called."

Sid said, "I'd rather be standing here than pacing around the apartment."

An hour passed. Sid sat on a stump; Oliver sat on the fallen tree beside her. He kept a wary eye out for Cole, whose voice made his blood boil.

A lot of grunting and panting drifted through the trees. But several holes in the earth had revealed nothing. He could hear Jameson discussing each before moving the officers, with their shovels, deeper into the woods. The voices became fainter with each change in location, and there was nothing for Oliver and Sid to see. It was frustrating.

Sid got up and brushed the dirt from her backside with an impatient sigh. "I'm going to pick some of these berries. I'm hungry."

"Serves you right. I had to throw out your perfectly nutritious breakfast." Oliver pulled her face down for a kiss before she slipped between the bushes.

When she was well away from him, their escort offered her name: Shannon. "I hear Sid is the woman this asshole abducted?"

"Yes." Oliver looked in Sid's general direction. "She's a real trooper. We only found her on Saturday."

Constable Shannon had leaned against a tree and opened her mouth to speak when Sid yelled from deep in the woods. Oliver and Shannon made eye contact and leaped into action.

"Where are you? Call us in, Sid."

"Here! Here! Here!"

Oliver homed in on her voice and reached her within seconds. She leaped into his arms, weeping. He held her and shook his head at Shannon, who stood with her hand on her sidearm as if a bear were about to attack.

Sid broke away from Oliver's arms and pointed to a large rectangular depression in the earth. "I was picking berries and needed to pee, so I came back here."

Shannon was on her radio. "Sergeant Jameson, I think Sidney may have found something. We're southeast of your position—off the trail about fifty meters."

After a few shouts, Jameson and the other officers were there. He walked around the depression, studying it. "Burns, get photos before we disturb it. Constable, when he's finished, clear the debris from around the edges and surface of the depression." He walked over to Sid and Oliver, who stood well back from the activity.

"This may well be it. What were you doing back here, Sid? Constable Shannon was supposed to keep an eye on you at the perimeter." He scowled at Oliver and threw a stern look at the constable.

Sid whispered, "I had to pee."

Jameson almost choked. He covered his mouth to hide his smile. "I won't mention that in my report."

"Thanks a lot." Sid looked around. "Are you going to bring Cole over here?"

"Not unless we find Alex's body."

Oliver wrapped his jacket around her, knowing she would snuggle back against him.

Jameson had just turned his attention back to the exhumation when Shannon said, "They're finished, Sergeant."

Two officers began to dig.

Jameson hovered around them, keeping his voice low. "Very shallow. Feel for resistance."

Oliver knew what that meant: bone. No one spoke. Labored breathing and blades slicing earth were the only sounds. The minutes felt like hours before the digging stopped.

The officers stood back and leaned on their shovels. "Sergeant."

Jameson kneeled at the edge of the exposed earth, reached in with a gloved hand, and swept the earth away from a skull.

Oliver's head spun. Dodging between officers, he fell to his knees at the edge of Alex's grave. He could not hear himself groaning in anguish. He could only feel his heart breaking.

* * *

MUFFLED voices and steady arms guided Oliver back to the car. He slumped in the passenger seat and stared into space.

In the distance, he heard Sid's voice. "Thanks, but I have some tranquilizers at home. I think I can get him into the apartment by myself."

Then, faintly, Jameson. "I'll call you later, but call me if you need help in the meantime."

The engine started, and Oliver's mind drifted back to the days, so many years ago, when he would walk through the park after school with Alex, his protector. How he wished someone had protected her.

At the apartment, Sid's voice filtered through his brain fog. "You have to walk under your own steam, Olly. Come on, put your feet on the ground. That's right. Here we go... We're almost there... Okay... We're home... Sit on the bed... Let's get your clothes off... That's it.

"Olly, sit up a little... Open your mouth... That's it... Now take a sip of this." She held a glass to his lips. "That's it."

He drifted off to a merciful sleep, hearing only Sid's heartbeat and feeling only the warmth of her body against his.

* * *

JAMESON'S VOICE infiltrated Oliver's dream. "How is he doing?"

"He's still asleep, thank goodness. I gave him one of my tranquilizers yesterday when we got home, and he's slept right through." ·

Have to get up. My pants. Oliver staggered into the other room.

Jameson caught his arm and guided him to the sofa. "Take it easy, Oliver."

"What are you doing here?"

"I came to see how you're doing."

"Not well, but I have to get up to Campbell River and tell the Renders we found Alex."

"Hold on a minute. We haven't confirmed that with DNA yet."

"The news will be out there long before you get DNA confirmation. It was Alex!" Oliver shouted. "I know it. I'm going before it leaks and they see it on the news."

"Well, I can't dissuade you, and you never listen to my orders anyway, so I guess it would be easier coming from you than a police officer. But promise me you will clarify that we have to do a DNA test to be absolutely certain." Jameson rose to leave.

Oliver nodded. "Sure."

When Sid saw him out, Jameson said, "Call me when you get back, okay?"

Sid assured him she would.

Oliver's stomach rumbled. He got up and poured himself a coffee. "I'd like to leave right after breakfast." He watched Alex spinning in his computer chair, and he knew... this might be the last time he saw her.

She smiled. *So... you're taking me home?*

* * *

ON THE DRIVE UP to Campbell River, Oliver and Sid stopped at the same beach and ate their lunch on a massive log weathered smooth from years of waves pounding against the shore.

Sid handed him a sandwich. "This is going to be harder than giving up Teddy, isn't it?"

"Thanks. And yes. You know... it's a funny thing. All the time we were looking for you, until yesterday, I never visualized Alex at all. But now I see her everywhere. It's as if I'm trying to hang on to her memory."

"I don't think there's any chance of you forgetting her. And you shouldn't want to."

Oliver drank the last of his water. "You're probably right." He pointed to the geese bobbing near the shore. "I see her feeding those geese like we used to do at the duck pond. Remember? She looks happy."

"A perfect memory, Olly. Let's get her home."

* * *

GLENDA AND ROB answered the door with hugs and tears. It was all Oliver could do to hold it together. Dabbing her eyes with a tissue, Glenda invited them in. "Have you had your lunch?"

"Yes, Glenda," said Sid. "We stopped on the beach at Shelter Bay."

"Well, I hope you saved room for some of Mother's chocolate cake." Rob plopped down in his threadbare recliner.

Oliver's eyes lit up. "Absolutely."

Glenda disappeared into the kitchen for a tray of coffee, plates, and forks. She carried the cake in with a pride that rivaled piping in the haggis.

With the last crumb pressed into his fork, Oliver took a deep breath. "I thought, when I first visited you, that if I ever made this trip, I'd feel better than I do. Alex has been an ever-present vision to me ever since the day she disappeared twelve years ago.

"Since I found that article, all I've wanted to do is to find her and bring her home. But not like this. Even after we knew the worst, I believed, when we found her, I would find peace for you and for me."

Rob leaned forward on his knees. "Son, we will all grieve again, but we will have closure now, and that will lessen the pain with time. We will never forget her, but our broken hearts will heal, and so will yours."

Sid squeezed Oliver's hand. "I think Oliver didn't expect to feel her loss so profoundly, so many years later."

Glenda took the family photo album from beneath the coffee table. She opened it, removed the last photo of Alex in the book, and handed it to Oliver. "You should have this."

Oliver cleared his throat and nodded. "Thank you. She looks just as I remember her, red scarf and all." He smiled when Alex kissed Glenda's cheek. And was it his imagination, or did Glenda just touch that cheek with her fingertips?

He rose to leave. "You'll probably be hearing from Sergeant Jameson soon, before it hits the news. And maybe the coroner. If you need me to help with any arrangements in Nanaimo, please just call."

"I will, Oliver dear. We are so grateful for all you've done to bring Alex home."

TWENTY-NINE

IT WAS SEPTEMBER ALREADY, and the days were getting cooler when Glenda and Rob held a memorial service for Alex in Nanaimo. Oliver didn't recognize any of her old classmates in attendance, but several came up to him and thanked him for finding her. Some remembered how much she had enjoyed his friendship.

Driving to the park, Sid remarked, "That was very sweet. That they remembered what a unique friendship you had."

Oliver held Alex's ashes on his knee. "Yes. Conveniently, they've forgotten how much they teased us back then."

Sid pulled the car in at the entrance to the park nearest the schoolyard. They walked the same path they had walked so many times over the years, this time with his fingers laced through Sid's. He stopped at the spot where Alex had hopped on the handlebars of his mind that day. "Well, Alex, I'm taking you from this spot to our favorite bench at the duck pond. Come on, Sid."

They sat on the bench until the sun sank beneath the trees and a cool breeze chased ripples across the pond.

Oliver opened the urn and scattered Alex's ashes to the wind.

* * *

LATER THAT EVENING, Oliver sat at his computer, staring at a blank document and a stack of dog-eared notebooks. *Where to begin?* When Oliver had shed Teddy, it was a relief at first... until he missed the little nuisance. But Alex was different. He'd gone through puberty with a huge crush on her, and after he and Sid became an item, Alex's jealousy seemed real. It didn't matter that she'd been killed twelve years before. His grief was genuine—as if it had just happened. Oliver felt an emptiness inside that he'd never felt before.

Sid massaged his neck. "Your grief is real, Oliver. Your pain is real. For you, she died only a month ago, not twelve years ago."

Oliver closed his eyes. "I wonder what my life would have been like if she had been found back then? Would I still see her? Would she look the way they found her? I shudder to think."

He looked up into Sid's soothing eyes. "I've got to do justice for Alex with this story." He pulled her around into his lap, buried his face in her neck, and wept.

Sid kissed his eyes and wiped the tears from his cheeks. "You will." She brushed the hair off his forehead. "I've got a confession to make that may motivate you."

Oliver closed one eye and warily searched her face with the other. "Oh, yeah?"

"Well... after you told me Professor Keegan gave you an extension on the assignment, I approached Professor Belland and requested an additional assignment to accompany your paper on Alex, since she was so much a part of our lives. Belland was enthusiastic and arranged for us to make a special presentation in an empty lecture hall for both professors—in a week."

Oliver's jaw dropped.

Sid kissed him and pointed at his monitor. "So? Hop to it."

* * *

OLIVER'S FINGERS flew over the keyboard.

As a reporter, I should not bring my personal feelings into this article, but forgive me while I tell you about my childhood friend, Alexis Young—a fifteen-year-old girl who befriended a bullied little boy of eight. She disappeared on the last day of school twelve years ago, only to be laid to rest today.

A week later, Oliver stood at the front of a lecture hall, loosening a collar that didn't exist as he adjusted the lectern to his height. "I want you to sit right here beside me during the reading, with your easel on your right."

Sid stood with her hands on her hips and nodded. "Okay. They'll be sitting in the front row so they can see it well."

Oliver rubbed his hands on his jeans. "Right. Should we keep it covered until I get to the part where she…?"

"Yes, I brought a drape. I can whip it off dramatically." Sid made an exaggerated sweep like a matador.

Right on time, the two professors arrived, and Sid directed them to their assigned seats.

Oliver nodded in their direction. "Welcome, Professors Keegan and Belland. Sidney Wheeler and I are extremely grateful for the opportunity to present our final assignments for last term. It is a collaboration that we hope you will find justifies the means."

Oliver began to read "The Story of Alex."

And from that moment on, he had their rapt attention.

With the requisite flair, Sid pulled the drape shrouding her canvas when he read, "From the moment she leaped onto the handlebars of my bike that fateful day…"

Oliver paused for a few moments when the professors stood and walked to the foot of the stage to examine *Friends on a Bicycle* more closely. On a path through an abstract wood, a boy pedals a bicycle away into the light. In front of him, a gossamer image of a girl bounces on the handlebars. Her feet, her long fair hair, and a long red scarf seem to float among sunbeams that stream through the trees.

As Oliver read Alex's obituary, Professor Keegan passed tissues to Professor Belland. Real men don't carry tissues, but apparently, they can still cry. A slow, hard clap came from the back of the lecture hall. Oliver strained to see who it was. The profs turned in their seats. It was Tom from the *Observer*. He strode down the aisle to the front.

"Now *that*, I would publish. Including the artwork." He shook hands with Keegan and Belland.

Professor Keegan was the first to regain her composure. "Well, Oliver and Sidney, I think we can unequivocally say you've passed... with a tardy slip."

* * *

AS THEY LOADED Sid's easel and painting into the car, Oliver shivered. It was the first time they had been in that lot since the day Cole kidnapped Sid. She was likely having the same thoughts, but Oliver didn't mention it. Why spoil a perfect day? Oliver grinned and drummed his fingers on the dash. "Let's stop off at Connie's and share this with her."

"She'd like that." Sid signaled the change in direction. "Connie told me how horrified she was when the news broke." Within minutes, Sid pulled up in front of the café.

"Take your painting in, Sid. The article needs it." Oliver stepped out into the afternoon sunshine, exhilarated.

Connie spotted them through the window and rushed to the door. "So, how did it go? By the grins on your faces, I'd say pretty good." She propped *Friends on a Bicycle* up on the counter for all to see. "That is so perfect, Sid." She motioned to a booth. "Sit, sit. What would you like? It's on the house today."

"Thanks, Connie. I think we should celebrate with a fancy coffee and some of your bumbleberry pie." Sid raised her eyebrows at Oliver. "Okay?"

"Sounds perfect." He handed Connie a copy of his article. "This is for you, Connie. Tom is going to publish it, but I'd like you to be the first to read it."

Connie plunked down on the bench beside him. "Oh, Oliver, I'm honored. Thank you." She wiped a tear from the corner of her eye and held his article against her chest. "I know you have done Alex justice. If it weren't for you, her murder would never have been discovered, and those two, who drank my coffee here for all those years, would have gotten away with it." With the sweep of her fingers, she wiped the scowl from her face and grinned. "Now let's get you that coffee and pie."

THIRTY

OLIVER PEERED out the windshield at the sky. "It's starting to rain. Let's swing by the library. I have a bunch of research material in my backpack to return. I also want to get a copy of the original article about Alex's disappearance. I gave mine to Jameson."

"Right. I think you should include that article with your essay."

Oliver squeezed her thigh. "My thoughts exactly."

They parked in the underground parkade of the convention center and made a dash across the plaza to the library, almost tripping over John's feet, which stretched out of the sheltering alcove. Oliver stooped and touched his shoulder. "You okay, John?"

John cleared the phlegm from his throat. "Never better, Oliver. Where's your bike?"

"Too wet for me. How's your suite at the Ritz coming along?"

"Nearly done. They say any day now. You two should come and spend some time there this winter." A violent hack wracked his lungs. "I'll show you the town."

Oliver palmed him a five-dollar bill. "Make us a reservation, and we'll be there."

"Straight up, Olly."

In the entrance, Oliver and Sid shook off the rain.

She raised an eyebrow in Oliver's direction. "What's this about the Ritz?"

"It's just a game we play so I can give him some money. I've seen him on the streets for years. A really nice guy. I'll bet there's a story there."

"You just bask in the glory of the one that's about to be published." She headed for the Arts section. "I'll find you when I'm done?"

Oliver kissed her. "That should hold me."

He was third in line to return his research material before taking the stairs to the mezzanine two at a time. *Good.* There was no one at the computer terminal where he'd first learned about Alex's disappearance. *It'll only take a minute.* He knew exactly where to find it. Within seconds, he was staring at the article again.

He glanced around—but no Alex spun on a computer chair or leaned against the stacks, twirling her scarf. He sighed.

Sid's hands ran down his chest when she rested her chin on his head. "I heard that sigh. Are you okay?"

He kissed her palm and pointed at the screen. "It's very sad, but not because the vivid memory I had of her all these years is gone. I look at that picture of her and I see a young girl whose life was cut short before it could even begin."

"But how do you feel about not seeing Alex anymore? You tried to get rid of her so often over the years, and now she's gone. Are you relieved? Or disappointed?"

Oliver stared at Alex's smiling face on the screen. "What do I feel? When we left her at the Renders', I was numb—numb with unexpected, overwhelming grief. I mean, you saw me at the memorial. I was a mess. But now I feel… privileged to have held her memory so strongly that I could help find her so many years later, after her life had been reduced to that article and a thin folder in the police cold-case files." Oliver fell silent. Minutes passed.

Just as he pressed print, his cell phone buzzed. He glanced around as he answered. "Jameson. What's up?"

"I think you'd better come down here, Oliver. A friend of yours has been brought in, and he's in pretty bad shape."

"A friend of mine? Who?"

"He says his name is John Doe, and he lists you as his next of kin."

Oliver poked the power button and dashed across to the printer. "I know him. We'll be right there."

Sid grabbed Oliver's backpack, and they swooped down the stairs and out into the rain. "They must have picked him up just minutes after we saw him."

Sid drove the few short blocks to the RCMP detachment, where Jameson met them at the door. An ambulance was pulling up. "Your friend is quite sick, Oliver. I'm sending him to the hospital."

The paramedics whisked past them to the cells, making Oliver's head swivel. "We just saw him a few minutes ago in front of the library. He listed me as his next of kin?"

Jameson ushered them into his office. "Yes. Isn't he?"

"No. I mean, he's a homeless man I've known for years. We have a passing friendly relationship, but that's it."

"Well, he insisted that we surrender his personal possessions to you in the event he dies." The door to Jameson's office was open, and the paramedics wheeled John past.

Oliver ran out and took John's hand. "Hey, John. I'll follow you to the hospital."

John's voice crackled. "Get my bag, Olly."

Oliver signed for John's satchel as the ambulance sped away. He shook Jameson's hand. "Thanks. I'll call you."

Sid sped away from the curb before Oliver could even buckle up. She pointed at the satchel—the kind a business executive might have used in the early nineteen hundreds. "What are you going to do with that?"

"I'm going to take it to him. Come on. Get behind that ambulance, Sid. This may contain identification and, who knows, maybe the lease to his suite at the Ritz." He clutched it to his chest, unable to manage even the feeblest of smiles.

When Sid pulled onto Terminal Avenue a half block behind the ambulance, Oliver pushed his foot to the floor and dug his nails into the dashboard. "Come on, John. Hang in there."

They were closing the gap when the siren fell silent. Oliver inhaled sharply. "He's died." For a moment, the windshield wipers and the tires on the wet road were the only sounds he heard.

Then, without warning, he bellowed, causing Sid to swerve.

"What's the matter with you? You look like you've seen a ghost."

Oliver tapped the rearview mirror with one trembling finger.

In the back seat... John Francis Doe hacked up more phlegm. "Don't lose that satchel, Oliver. I'm counting on you. There's a story there."

The End except for....

MY THANKS to you for reading *Killing Imaginary Friends*. I hope you enjoyed Oliver's quest for peace, freedom, and justice. Even though he thought of them as a burden, I think Teddy and Alex helped Olly become Oliver, the self-confident, compassionate man he is today. What do you think? If you enjoyed *Killing Imaginary Friends*, please leave a review on BookBub, Goodreads, Books2Read or wherever you purchased *Killing Imaginary Friends*.

In my imaginary world, the inspiration for *Killing Imaginary Friends* occurred to me when I realized some faces and images have stuck with me my whole life, especially if they are linked to a traumatic event. Not that I would call myself a face recognizer by any means, but during my research, I found the phenomenon intriguing. So I've played with this ability and allowed Olly, under stress, to visualize his imaginary friends.

To keep apprised of my progress on the next book in the Oliver Frampton Mystery series, sign up for my newsletter at https://ardelleholden.com/. "There's a story there," in John Francis Doe's satchel.

X x.com/AuthorHolden

instagram.com/ardelleholden.author.artist

pinterest.com/ardelleholden

OTHER BOOKS BY ARDELLE HOLDEN

THE SAMANTHA BOWERS MYSTERIES – A TRILOGY

A PERSON OF INTEREST

A Duplicity of Treachery and Deception

Samantha's pulse raged. Could they hear it from down the alley? She hesitated, held her breath, and listened. In the darkness, pelting rain muffled the voices of the two men she knew would soon round the corner and see her silhouetted against the light from the street beyond. Ahead, she spotted the dark recess of a delivery entrance.

As her mind raced, Samantha's feet struggled in nightmarish slow motion against the grip of debris and rushing water that conspired to drag her backwards into danger. The instant she reached the doorway, she leaped onto the threshold. Pressing her back hard against the ridges of the cold metal door, she wished she could melt into it like a Dali watch.

MURDER BY BITS AND BYTES

A Conspiracy of Greed and Ruthless Revenge

Samantha showered in the glow of anticipation of this romantic getaway weekend. How could she know she would spend it alone? It seemed nothing would keep the memory of murder and terror buried in the cellar of her mind.

Ben had promised to unplug this weekend—he would leave the Bach House Vineyards IT project at the office. When he glanced at the wine and flowers on the passenger seat with his computer bag, he couldn't help but grin, knowing he would arrive at the cottage well before Sam, with time to get the fireplace crackling and the chill off the sheets. He would soon wish he had kept his promise.

MURDER BY PINS AND NEEDLES

The Life and Death of Love, Loyalty, and Betrayal

Until she saw the horror on Ben's face, it hadn't occurred to Samantha that a menacing murder of crows had congregated in this *Attic Windows* quilt. It gave her pause to examine it more closely, and what she discovered gave her chills. Who was this woman, L. Bennett, so tormented by suspicion that she hid clues to her own murder in a quilt for her son, Nicky? Or was it a daughter? Was she murdered, or is she alive, steeped in paranoia?

ACKNOWLEDGMENTS

In the real world, Donna Barker, Eileen Cook, Crystal Hunt, Stephanie Candiago, and the members of the Creative Academy for Writers have been my mentors and cheerleaders. Seven days a week, they provide me with hours of online sprints, master classes, guest presenters, advice, technical support, and companionship. I am so fortunate to have met my extraordinary editor, Amanda Bidnall, through the Creative Academy. She gave me the confidence to type "The End."

But most of all, I thank you, dear reader. I write for you.

Sincerely,

Ardelle Holden

ABOUT THE AUTHOR

My husband, Patrick, and I raised our two children while adventuring in aviation, mining exploration, and the wild rice lakes of Northern Manitoba. In Lac du Bonnet, I opened the Country Mouse Scrapbooker on the farm. In Victoria, I worked as a medical office assistant, a videographer of family albums, and a seamstress for well-coordinated square dancers. Now, Vancouver Island is home. I enjoy glorious sunsets over Quennell Lake and Mount Benson. It's a perfect spot for writing. In Mexico in the winter, the views of Mount Garcia over Lake Chapala provide another quiet scene conducive to writing and other artistic pursuits.

In all this tranquility, I'll bet you are wondering where all the murder and mayhem comes from. It's in those tranquil moments that my imagination roams free and finds its way onto the pages of my novels.

https://ardelleholden.com/